FOR MAISIE—I REMEMBER.

PROLOGUE

Have you ever been to the mountains of West Virginia? Have you ever sat on a porch in the hills there on an early summer night, when the air is so soft and clean that it seems like you can smell the jasmine for miles? Have you ever watched the sun rise over a West Virginia mountain lake, making steam come off the water like smoke?

If you have, then you know that the place where I was born, under the shadow of the biggest mountains east of Tennessee, in a mountain range called the Appalachians, is sometimes the closest thing to heaven you can imagine. It used to be more than that to me. It used to be home.

My name is Glory Mason. I know, strange name, Glory. My parents were so happy when my mama finally popped me out, they named me something that would always remind them of how thankful they were to God. That was when they were still my parents. Before they decided I wasn't their daughter anymore.

I guess you could say I've lost my life. The people I knew growing up consider me dead. My mama and daddy, my brother and sisters—they consider me dead, too. They're part of my past, and I'm part of theirs. I'm only a ghost now.

Sometimes I stare up at the moon like I used to back home

and think about things like the universe and how all those stars just keep going forever and ever, until you wonder if somewhere out there is just a huge block of white hiding behind a big black cloth with pinholes in it. More often, though, I think about Dogwood. And I wonder, does it ever occur to the folks back home that I'm not really dead at all?

Oh, I'm sure Mama knows that I'm somewhere out in the world trying to look after myself. And Theo and Teresa probably wonder where I might be. But what about Reverend Clifton? What about the little ones? They're too young to know any better. Do folks tell them I'm dead?

I wouldn't blame them for believing it. Like I said, in a way, I *am* dead.

But in a more important way, I'm alive. I'm alive to myself. And even though I know I won't be around for very much longer, I still have a little time to see what the world is all about. So a while ago, I decided something important—that I'm not going to spend the rest of my time wishing I were already gone. I'm not going to spend it begging my family to take me back when I know they never will. I'm going to see what it's like out there.

My folks tried to keep it from me. My daddy told me that the world beyond Dogwood is corrupt, that outsiders are greedy and careless, that their laws were made for *their* benefit and not for people like us. But I know different stories. Better stories. There's a world beyond the world I know, and I'm going to be part of it before I die.

CHAPTER ONE

Clang!

The loud noise jarred me awake, pulling me out of the lovely dream I was having. I kept my eyes squeezed shut and tried to go back to sleep, hoping to recapture the dream—even though it had never worked before.

Clang! Clang! Clang!

The morning before Thanksgiving my attempts were hopeless as usual. Daddy was banging away on the coal furnace pipes like a demon, and I knew there was no way he was going to stop until he was sure he'd made enough noise to wake me and the rest of the lazy world.

Sighing, I sat up in bed and leaned over to light a candle, my breath puffing out into the air in front of me. Lord, I hated getting up on cold mornings. Going to bed on cold nights was different 'cause the covers were cozy and Mama always had the furnace lit until us children went to sleep, but mornings—well, they weren't for me. The sound of my daddy's footsteps clumping across the kitchen floor below told me he figured he'd made enough noise. The front door slammed shut behind him, and through the filmy glass of my bedroom window I made out his tall frame heading across the grass toward the barn lot.

I scooted off the bed with a squeak and padded across the room, shivering. The morning light filtering in meant I was already late for my chores, which were supposed to start at daybreak. And judging by the lingering smell of eggs and coffee drifting up the stairs, I figured that breakfast had come and gone.

I opened the wardrobe at the far end of my room and pulled out a shirt, a pair of coveralls, wool socks, leather boots. Except for the coveralls and the boots, my mama had sewn, knitted, or patched all these clothes together for me herself. The boots had been made by Ezekiel Brown, our town cobbler. The coveralls had come secondhand from somewhere outside of town. They'd been my brother Theo's until he outgrew them, and I'd snagged them before Mama could give them away. I changed into them, yanked my dark hair into a ponytail, and slipped it through a bauble my best friend, Katie, had given me for my birthday. Then I headed downstairs.

Sure enough, though the lamp was still burning in the middle of the kitchen table, no one was about and breakfast was gone. I knew there was more in the icebox, but I'd have to cook it myself, and Daddy would have a fit if I weren't up in the barn feeding the horses soon. I reached into the cupboard and pulled out a couple of stale biscuits. I stuffed one into my pocket and gnawed on the other as I headed for the coffeepot and poured the last drops into a cup, slurping the coffee down before making my way out the front door.

Despite the cold, it was a beautiful morning. The fields were glowing and crackling with frost, and the sunrise was rust colored on the horizon. I could see other folks in the fields—Mr. Taylor, Eric Jackson, my uncle Andrew—already hard at work on their chores, welcoming the new day and making the most of it.

Daddy and Theo, my older brother, were up by the harness room on the side of the barn, and after a quick trip to the outhouse, that's where I headed.

"Morning," Daddy said, not lifting his eyes from what he was doing but knowing I was there all the same. I perched myself on the fence.

"Morning, Daddy. Morning, Theo."

My brother shrugged in my direction. Daddy was sharpening an ax, and Theo had his hands fisted tightly around a sack that bulged and kicked and gobbled. I knew with a queasy feeling that Theo had just caught a turkey and that they were about to slaughter it for the next day's big Thanksgiving supper. Poor turkey.

"I'm sorry you couldn't join us for breakfast this morning, Glory." Daddy threw me a stern glance. "I reckon your ma and sister have been spoiling you, letting you sleep so late—you're old enough to get up with the rest of us." His left hand gripped the handle of the ax as he ground it against the whetstone. "Theo, just tie up that turkey and leave it here. Edgar said he'd need you at the forge this morning, but before that I need you to go down to the White place and . . ." Daddy went on for a minute, talking about whatever boring town-leader business he was sending Theo to take care of. Usually he handled all that stuff himself, but like he sometimes said, "I only have two hands."

Daddy finished with the ax and straightened up to his full height. If I didn't know my daddy, I would've thought he looked kind of scary standing there—a tall, burly man with black hair and dark, flashing eyes, getting ready to slaughter a turkey. He turned his attention back to me. "By much slothfulness the building decayeth; and—"

"—through idleness of the hands the house droppeth through," I finished. "I know. I'm up, aren't I?" It wasn't the first time he'd quoted me this verse about sloth and idleness, which are just fancy Bible words for being lazy, but I guess he'd forgotten how many times. "I can't help it if my dreams are so interesting that they're harder to wake up from than everybody else's," I said with a grin.

Theo, who was hanging around, probably to see if I was going to get punished, rolled his eyes at me. I ignored him. Sliding off the fence, I caught at the left shoulder-strap of Daddy's coveralls, which was undone. "It's too bad the Bible doesn't say anything about dressing, 'cause then I could quote *you* a verse or two." Daddy's mouth stayed firm, but his eyes looked amused and, glancing down at his appearance, a little embarrassed. Despite all his strictness and smart sayings, he was, in a word, unruly—from his unruly black hair, to his unruly whiskers, to his unruly clothing that always looked like he'd worn it to bed. Which would, in fact, be a good description of me, too—only without the whiskers.

"Don't sass me, Glory," he said. His eyes lost their twinkle. "It's not just sleeping late that's the problem. It's your attitude. All the childish mischief and such." He paused. "You're thirteen years old as of last week—only two years younger'n your mama was when she and I got married. You're a woman now, and you need to start acting like one."

I thought of the childish mischief he was referring to. Most recently that included talking back to the Reverend, whacking Thomas Johansen with a stick when he tried to kiss me, and falling in the creek in my Sunday dress and getting it covered with mud when I was supposed to be helping cook dinner. They were all far from mortal sins but a little more serious for the daughter of the town leader than for others, I guessed.

"Yeah, so maybe you should just go on back to the house and do the laundry with the other women," Theo chimed in, which was a jab at me because he knew I hated stuff like mending and washing and housework and much preferred being out in the barn or the fields. Theo was always too bent on impressing Daddy to ever say what was really on his mind, so I guessed he was just jealous of my outspokenness.

"That's enough, Theo. Run along to the Whites'," Daddy said.

I threw Theo a dirty look as he trudged away, then turned back to my father.

"Could be I've been a bit too soft on you, Glory," Daddy continued. "You need to start learning the responsibilities of being a woman." He glanced at my coveralls and frowned. "Including wearing a proper dress."

I just stared at my fingernails. It was so unfair, calling me a woman and telling me I had to stop getting into mischief when Theo still got into loads of mischief and didn't get into trouble at all because he was *male.* And the coveralls—Daddy knew it was easier to work in pants than a dress!

But there was no point in arguing. Daddy had been on about the woman stuff recently, and it wasn't open to discussion. God, morals, sometimes even a little gossip—those things I could talk with Daddy about and he'd hear me out just like he would any grown person. At least, he used to. But the woman stuff . . . well, when it came to that, I could forget about trying to change his mind.

"You hear me, Glory?"

"Yes, sir, I hear you," I said halfheartedly.

"Good," Daddy said. His face softened, and he almost looked a little sorry. He let out a sigh. "You're always so good at things when you put your mind to them. Like arguing"—he smirked—"and school. You need to put your mind to this, too."

He was looking at me earnestly, but I wasn't paying attention anymore. "School!" I blurted, clapping my hands to my mouth. That was all I said before I turned on my heel and started running. "Can you please ask Theo to feed the horses?" I yelled back over my shoulder. "I'm late!"

A last look backward showed Daddy just shaking his head. It was an I-give-up kind of shake. But I couldn't think about that now—about whether he was going to let it slide or punish me later. All I knew was that I was supposed to be somewhere else. And I was supposed to be there hours ago!

Our schoolhouse wasn't really a schoolhouse at all, but an extra room, a later addition that stuck out of the church building and looked as out of place as a giant mole poking out of someone's face. Like the mole that I was staring at that very moment on the Reverend's left nostril. I tried to pay attention to what he was saying because he sure was mad, but that mole always made me think of stuff like the way the schoolroom looked poking out of the side of the church and whether or not hair would grow out of it when the Reverend got older (the mole, not the schoolroom).

So I just kept nodding, and the Reverend kept talking. He was pointing to the inscription above the blackboard at the back of the room: "'The foolishness of man perverteth his way; and his heart fretteth against the Lord'—Proverbs 19:3." I didn't see what that had to do with anything. I wasn't fretting against the Lord. I was just late.

"You, Miss Glory Mason, are a lollygagger, a daydreamer, and a do-less. The petty crimes you commit today are going to turn into tomorrow's sin. The Lord frowns on your irresponsibility." The Reverend waved his finger in front of my face and then used it to draw attention to his wristwatch—the only one in town. "You are to be here at six-thirty sharp to prepare for lessons. No exceptions. You hear me?" I nodded and tried to look as sorry as I could. But I wasn't all that sorry.

I was supposed to help the Reverend with school every Wednesday, from just after dawn until three o'clock in the afternoon, because when I was a student, I'd been a good one, and also because I was the town leader's daughter and supposed to set an example. I'd been doing it for about five months now, but I supposed I couldn't really count my time as five full months since I'd been late so often.

I took the podium at the front of the room, underneath a small wooden cross on the wall, as the Reverend gathered up his things in a huff. Wednesdays were his days to call on all the people of Dogwood, say prayers and make blessings, give advice on questions of right and wrong, and so on. It was sort of like what my daddy did all the time as town leader, only a lot holier. I was supposed to teach lessons based on an outline he'd made. That day the outline looked something like this:

Prayer
History
Arithmetic
Religion
Prayer
Reading/Writing

I'd already missed the first prayer, and the Reverend's book was open to the middle of the history lesson.

"Hi, y'all." I looked around the room and grinned at the students, eighteen kids between the ages of five and eleven. They all looked scrubbed and starched . . . and relieved. I knew from experience that I was a welcome break from the Reverend and his droning voice.

"Hi, Miss Glory," came the reply. I squirmed. I'd been sitting in the place of those kids just a couple of short years ago, calling my big sister, Teresa, "Miss" when she was the teacher, and it was hard getting used to that "Miss" being me. The closet in the back of the room was engraved with my and Katie's initials. The back corner by the coat hooks had been scuffed more than enough times by my very own shoes when I was sent to stand there for making trouble.

"Okay, let's see," I said, looking at the page before me and smoothing out the edges. Like most of our books, this one was handwritten, inscribed ages ago, and the ink was starting to blur from old age.

" 'When they saw that the new world of America was corrupt,' " I read, " 'Jonas Wilkerson and his fellow believers decided to make a *new* new world—one that was governed not by the laws of man, but of God. Times were hard at first, but it is thanks to these brave Christians that the town of Dogwood was formed in 1871. Here we are faithful to the belief that men should have the right to protect their families, that women should serve their men and their families in the way that God intended, and that children should be raised to bow to no ruler except for Jesus Christ, their Lord.' "

I paused, annoyed with the part about women serving men, which I knew really meant doing the boring indoors work and acting like men knew more than them. Looking up, I saw that Lyle Johansen, Katie's little brother, had his hand raised.

"Lyle?"

"Was Jonas Wilkerson one of Jesus' apostles?" he asked.

I suppressed a smile. Most children in Dogwood knew the story of its beginning backwards and forwards, partly because it was repeated in school every year right before Thanksgiving. The point was to teach us young people why we should give thanks for everything we have, and especially for the wisdom of our ancestors in creating Dogwood for us true Christians. But more than that, in Dogwood, history was everything. The *history* of our ancestors. The *history* of the Bible. The *history* of our village. Daddy always said our history was what made us who we were.

"Nah, Jonas Wilkerson wasn't one of the apostles. He was pretty holy, though. And very serious. Just look." I held up the book so everyone could see the old lithograph pasted to the left-hand side—a shriveled, bearded little man dressed all in black, his mouth turned down in a scowl.

I turned the page and kept reading out loud—all about the evils of the outside world and all the modern conveniences steering everyone away from hard work and self-discipline— "contraptions you could never even dream of" that were "the devil's hand tools."

"Well, no matter how evil the world is," I added, "I sure would like to get my hands on one or two of those amazing contraptions. Maybe they have machines that do housework for you." Some kids muttered agreement or giggled.

"And they have those cars where the tops come off," Carrine Jackson piped in. "Thomas told me."

"Oh, you'll believe anything you hear," Carrine's brother Matthew muttered, and a few of the children tittered.

"No, it's true," Jane Taylor piped up. "It really is, Matthew. And they *do* have contraptions that do housework for you. Like for washing clothes. And one to fold them, too."

The class erupted in a debate, with everyone arguing what did and did not really exist in the outside world—and everyone trying to top each other with fantastical ideas about what things were like in other, modern towns. Televisions definitely existed. Spaceships, too. Machines that washed clothes—that was a tougher one, and the class was divided.

When the Reverend came back around half-past two, the classroom was in chaos. Little Lily White was running around pretending to be an airplane, her arms spread out to demonstrate, and Lyle Johansen was standing on his desk chair, saying he was in the circus. I had my hand over my stomach, laughing.

I was the first to notice the Reverend standing there in the doorway. His nostrils were flaring out with each breath, so that he looked like an angry bull—a bull with a mole on his nose. As the children caught sight of him, the whole class fell silent. I braced myself for a lecture.

But I reckon the Reverend couldn't stand to deal with me anymore, because he simply stood with his back to the door and motioned for me to leave. Which was fine by me since usually he had me stick around and do chores, like wiping down the blackboards. Grateful to head outdoors again and unaffected by the Reverend's sourness, I waved good-bye to the class and gave them a sympathetic smile. Then I walked into the November sunshine.

Out on the porch, I pulled on my sweater, noticing a dark spot on the doorsill as I did. *Oh.* With a sinking feeling, I leaned closer to get a better look at it—a black woolly worm. I'm not all that superstitious, but Mama says black woolly worms mean an extra-long winter is on the way.

I held the tip of my finger next to the caterpillar and watched it crawl slowly onto my fingernail, its sticky little feet moving two by two. Then I lowered it onto a nearby plant.

I sighed and looked around. The day was beautiful. The breeze was cool but soft. I couldn't imagine winter coming at all, ever.

I took a deep breath of November air and began my walk home.

CHAPTER
TWO

How can I tell you what home looks like in my mind's eye? How can I tell you what it smells like when the leaves are turning dry or when it's just rained? How can I show you why it's tied to my heart in every way and how every wood-framed, crooked little house and cozy hiding place and stretch of path seems more precious to me than gold?

The village of Dogwood is perched on top of a hill that on one side slopes into a woodsy valley with a beautiful lake, and on another tilts up toward the Appalachian Mountains. The houses, all one- or two-story affairs, all built by hand, are clustered pretty much in one area at the edge of the fields of wheat and corn. They're all connected by worn dirt paths that lead from house to house, to the church, to the dairy, to the forge, and way down to the town supply shed.

It was planned that way, connected like that, because while every family has their own house, everything else is shared—from the milk to the wool to the vegetables. Everybody works together and shares the food they grow, which is the way Jonas Wilkerson wanted it, I guess, and which makes a lot of sense because the town is so small, everybody is like family. There are only about sixty people in Dogwood, and most are related to each other somehow—and even if they're not, they act like they are.

On that day, the whole town and the hills beyond were painted with flaming splotches of red, orange, and brown. I walked down the dirt path that led out of the schoolroom, around the left side of the church, and out into the field beyond. Below and around me, the town was in full swing. Since all of Dogwood is on a hillside and the church is perched far above the rest of the buildings, I could see everything under the sun from where I was standing. Or at least, every part of Dogwood—the only thing under the sun for me. It was a shame to have to head home on a day like this.

Katie usually came over on Wednesday afternoons, so I headed downhill to her house, figuring I could walk with her. Mrs. Johansen, Katie's mama, was sitting on her front porch, snapping peas.

"Good afternoon, Glory Bee," she said, shading her eyes with her left hand to watch my approach. "Reverend let you out a little early, did he?"

I smiled dryly. Mrs. Johansen was about my favorite person in the whole world, next to her daughter, and one of the few adults in town who wasn't always looking at me like I was a rotten apple. "I don't think he could stand to be around me one more minute than he had to. He was sore at me when I came in and even sorer at me when I left."

She gave a soft laugh. "Well, more time for you to come inside and talk to me while Katie finishes her upstairs chores. I was just about done with these peas." She got up and gathered the peas in her apron. I climbed the porch stairs and followed her inside through the squeaky screen door, trailing behind little Zeke, whose hands were buried in the folds of his mother's dress.

As usual, I basked in the warm, otherworldly dimness of Katie's house—which Mr. Johansen had built special for his wife before they got married. Mrs. Johansen was the only person who lived in Dogwood who hadn't been born and raised there. She grew up in Wellsburg, a town about fifty times the size of Dogwood, and her husband-to-be had claimed that a sophisticated lady like her needed an extra-special house to feel at home in. A few of the older folks in town thought the house was too extravagant, with fancy gingerbread latticework on the eaves—which, according to folks, was unnecessary—extra counters and cabinets in the kitchen, and the like. But I thought it was wonderful.

Mrs. Johansen tugged my ponytail affectionately. "That," she said, nodding to the basket filled with husked corn and peeled sweet potatoes sitting on the kitchen counter, "is for your mother. The least she can do is let me peel and shuck a few vegetables for her."

I nodded and pulled up a seat at the kitchen table as she put an envelope down in front of me.

"And *this*," she said, darting her eyes sideways, as if to tell me she was about to let me in on a secret, and then nodding at the envelope, "is for you. To look at, anyway. It showed up in the attic the other morning." She filled a mug with hot cider and then sat down beside me.

I pulled out the contents slowly, carefully. It was a single photograph—of a little girl standing in front of a brick building. A church, it looked like. The girl's hands were in white gloves, and she was wearing a beautiful dress covered in flowers. Beside her, an old lady stood beaming into the camera.

"Is this you?" I asked.

Mrs. Johansen smiled. "Me and my grandma. That's the church she used to take me to when I visited her in Boston. This was taken right after we got out." She let out a little laugh. "After church, we used to go to a pastry shop around the corner, called Vincent's, so you can see how happy I was. My grandma and me—we both loved those fancy pastries." A sad little smile crossed her face, and then she cleared her throat.

"I found it when I was up in the attic, looking for my old spice rack. Katie just enjoyed it so much when I showed it to her, and we were sure you would, too."

I nodded again and went back to studying the picture. Beyond the edges of the church steeple, the sky was as clear as it could be. The palm of someone's hand had made its way onto the left edge. I stared at the photo hard, trying to memorize the whole thing so I could add to it with my imagination later.

Katie and I liked to look at Mrs. Johansen's old pictures from time to time and dream about what the places were like just beyond the edges of the photos. She only had a few that she'd saved when she moved to Dogwood, but that was enough because Katie and I could imagine the rest. Most of all we liked to picture Boston: the fancy tall buildings and the park with ducks and little boats and the tree-lined streets and all the cars, just like Mrs. Johansen had described it. When we were smaller, we even used to pretend to eat in the fancy restaurants where strangers cooked for you, and we'd make Mrs. Johansen describe every meal she could remember having to the point where we could almost taste it ourselves.

Of course, we always did this stuff in secret because Katie's mama would surely get in trouble with her husband for encouraging our idle fancies, maybe even opening our minds to sin. But she knew how happy it made us. She knew that to Katie and me, Boston and the rest of the world seemed too good to be real. And honestly, how could it be all that bad if Mrs. Johansen had come from it and turned out to be so kind and mannerly and nice?

"It's lovely," I said, tucking the picture back in the envelope. "Thank you for showing it to me. Your grandma must've been nice, huh?"

Mrs. Johansen opened her mouth to answer, but before she could, footsteps sounded on the wooden stairs, and then Katie was in the kitchen beside me. "Hi," she said as she squeezed my hand, standing there in her neat calico dress with the same gentle smile her mama had. The same tiny, delicate bone structure. The same long, deerlike legs. How a dainty lady like Mrs. Johansen had given birth to seven boys I did not know, but Katie was a living reminder that her mama was a genuinely feminine female.

"There's my girl," Mrs. Johansen said, catching Katie by the waist and pulling her to her side to kiss her cheek. "Now, you be sure to help Mrs. Mason like you're supposed to. I know you two, and it's likely you'll do more giggling than chores if you don't stay on top of yourselves." With that she patted Katie's back to dismiss her and gave me a glance that was meant to say, "I mean business," but really said, "I think you're both wonderful no matter what." I got up, and Katie took up the vegetable basket in her arms.

"Tell your mama not to hesitate to call on me if she needs any help."

I nodded, even though we both knew that Mama would never do so. She was too much the perfect hostess, too conscious of being the town leader's wife to let Mrs. Johansen lift a finger to help with tomorrow's Thanksgiving meal—even though it would be both our families that were eating it. Katie's family and mine shared Thanksgiving, I guess because Mr. Johansen was like my daddy's second in command. Which was fine by me because I liked all the Johansens, all ten of them—with the exception of Thomas, who was always trying to get me to kiss him.

Katie and I headed out the door and down the main path

toward home, sharing the burden of the basket, which was a bit too heavy for Katie. As always, I imagined that Katie and I looked quite a pair walking around town, with all her delicateness beside all my unruliness and my angular frame and straight features. But I kind of liked it, too—feeling like I was her protector. It made me feel like I was making up for the fact that she always somehow managed to get her chores done in half the time I did so she could come over to help me with mine. It was a blessing because even though I had to help at the school, I was supposed to do all the day's chores no matter what.

As we walked, Katie and I stopped every once in a while to chat and exchange hellos with our neighbors while they worked in their fields and gardens and got ready for Thanksgiving. Several of the older folks gave Katie warm smiles and greetings before turning to me doubtful expressions and tight little *hellos*. In Dogwood, everyone knows everyone else so well that it's like having twenty parents instead of two, and they all know when you've been good or bad and take it as their responsibility to rear you up right. So even when I wasn't up to mischief, folks gave me looks that said, "You better be behaving yourself, Glory Bee Mason."

"Well, well, Miss Tardy. What do you have to say for yourself?" Speak of the devil. I turned to see Mrs. White, who'd just emerged onto her porch. She was standing with her arms crossed and staring at me over her little square glasses.

"Good afternoon, Mrs. White," Katie and I both replied.

"Hello, Katie," she said, nodding to Katie with a tiny smile, then turning back to me with a scowl. "The Reverend was late for our prayer breakfast this morning, and I hear it was on account of your irresponsibility."

A snappy reply came to my mind, but Katie nudged me in the ribs, and I decided to hold my tongue. "Yes, Mrs. White," I said. Still, it hadn't come across sounding as polite as I'd hoped.

"Don't sass me, girl. You know how the Lord feels about punctuality."

That made me mad. "I don't remember anything in the Bible about punctuality," I said as sweetly as I could. "But I'll be sure to look it up. What verse do you mean, Mrs. White?"

Mrs. White's neck turned red, just like a turkey cock's. "You'd best take care, Glory Bee Mason," she said angrily. "You're starting down a bad road. Lance King used to sass folks the way you do—and you know how he ended up!"

Before I could reply, Katie grabbed my hand and pulled me along, leaving crabby old Mrs. White to stare after us.

"I am so sick of people telling me I'm going to end up like Lance King," I muttered. "I mean, he was bad, Katie. *Really* bad. Wasn't he?"

Katie squeezed my fingers. "Of course he was, Glory," she said stoutly. "Mrs. White was just talking, that's all."

The fact was, none of us children really knew what all Lance King had done. All I knew was what us children were told: that he'd been cast out of Dogwood when he was only sixteen years old. Folks talked about him like he'd been the devil himself.

Casting out is the worst punishment you can get in Dogwood. It's only happened four times since the town was founded. It's another part of our history, a dark part. How it works is, the entire town meets and decides you're no longer fit to live, and they send you away into the mountains. But first they make you drink the Water of Judgment, which isn't really water at all but some stuff that the Reverend keeps in a brass vial locked up behind the altar. Nobody really knows what's in the Water of Judgment. Some folks say it's made out of snake venom. After you drink it, they say it stays inside you for about a year, floating around in your blood, killing you bit by bit.

Some people die sooner, though. They found Lance King's body not ten miles from town, just three weeks after he was cast out. I was only four or five, but I still remember how his mama cried like a wild animal when she heard.

"Mrs. White was just talking," Katie said again.

"I know," I told her. But I felt like some of the beauty had gone out of the day.

"I don't know what she's so high and mighty about, anyway," I said after a few moments, "when everyone knows she has one of those corn pipes hidden in her house somewhere and smokes it when Mr. White's laid up in bed."

Katie's eyes widened. "No!"

"Yes, you didn't know?" I nodded vigorously for emphasis. "Theo saw her with his own eyes out on her screen porch doin' it just the other night, and he said she hid it under her skirt real quick when she saw him and almost lit herself on fire."

"Glory, you're lying!"

"It's the truth," I said, not really knowing whether it was or wasn't. Theo had just said he'd smelled smoke coming from the porch where Mrs. White was standing, and I'd kind of filled in the rest. But it sounded right to me, and besides, Katie seemed so impressed. And it served Mrs. White right for saying I'd end up like Lance King. It was an awful thing to tell anyone. And then there she was, virtually caught in the act of committing a sin like smoking tobacco, which was almost as evil as drinking spirits.

Katie walked on in silence. "I suppose she needs something to get her through the day with Mr. White being so sick and all," she said after a few moments. That was Katie for you—always excusing everybody for everything.

"Well, if she's smoking to help her get through tough times, she must've started the day she married him, right before she had to kiss him."

"Glory!" Katie said, looking scandalized, but she couldn't suppress a smile. "Don't be mean!" We both knew Mr. White was the homeliest, grumpiest man in Dogwood, on top of having a clubfoot, and that Mrs. White (who wasn't any prize, either) had married him because he was the only one in town near her age who wasn't already hitched or engaged.

I scrunched up my face and held up one foot with my left hand, imitating Mr. White's clubfoot, hopping along. "Kiss me, my love!" I said, leaning toward Katie, who snorted with laughter and quickly covered her mouth.

"Glory, quit it!"

Not looking where I was going, I kept hopping until I fell over, grabbing Katie's arm for balance and pulling her down with me. "Kiss me, darlin', kiss me!" Katie toppled over me onto the dirt path, and I gave her a loud slobbery kiss on the cheek. We were a tangle of calico and coveralls and legs and hair.

Suddenly I felt that feeling of someone being very close by and looked up. *Oh.* There was my daddy, standing above me, his hands on his hips and Eric Jackson by his side. *Uh-oh.* For a moment I thought he was going to laugh, but he was dead silent. I thought about the talk we'd had this morning and gulped.

"Hi, Daddy, hi, Mr. Jackson," I said, jumping up and brushing myself off. Katie shot up beside me and adjusted her bun.

Daddy said nothing—he just turned to Mr. Jackson. "I'm sorry, Eric, that my daughter has the manners of a billy goat. Glory," he said, facing me again. "I'll talk with you about your behavior when I get home."

I felt my ears go red. It wasn't what he'd said so much. It was the way he'd looked at me—like someone he didn't know or didn't like. "I'm sorry, Daddy, I was just . . ." But I trailed off because he wasn't looking at me anymore. He was talking to Mr. Jackson.

"Sounds to me, Eric, like she hasn't been milked enough, and now her udders are too swollen to produce properly. Go talk to Len White and see if he can spare Michael to help out with that. If he can't, let me know and I'll send Theo over."

"Hey, Daddy," I said, wanting to make him smile. "You'll never guess what Lyle said in class today. Mr. Jackson, you'll like this, too. I was talking about—"

My father turned on me, his eyes dark and flashing.

"Glory! I'm talking to Mr. Jackson."

"Yes, but—"

"Enough. We'll need to have a long talk about your manners when I get home. Now go on."

I felt a lump rise in my throat. Katie looked mortified.

"I'm going," I muttered, trying not to sound as hurt as I felt.

It was no use, anyway, because he didn't even hear. Katie and I started down the path again in silence. I kicked at a leaf, and when I missed, I pulled my foot back and stomped on it.

"It's okay, Glory," Katie said, putting a delicate hand on my shoulder. "He's just busy, that's all."

"Oh, I don't care." I made my voice high to make sure I sounded like I meant it. "I'm sure that sick cow is really important."

"It's not the cow, Glory," Katie said. "He's just doing what he needs to do, you know, as leader. My daddy is the same way sometimes. He wants you to be a good example because you're becoming an adult."

I nodded agreement, but it wasn't as bad with Katie's daddy as it was with mine. At least Katie's daddy could be proud of her, on account of her being so perfect. For my daddy, it seemed like I was a big disappointment. At least these days it did.

"I don't see how I can walk around on this earth and not mess up at all," I said, my voice cracking. "It's like he doesn't even want me to be *me* anymore."

"Oh, Glory, you're wrong," Katie said, wrapping her arm around my neck and pulling me close for a sideways hug. "The person you are is wonderful. I'm sure your daddy knows that."

"Well, he could do a better job of showing it," I said.

When we got to my house, I was still in a foul mood. And it only got fouler when I saw Reverend Clifton sitting at our kitchen table with Theo. Ugh. He'd beaten us home.

"If you ask me, Thanksgiving has become too much about eating and too little about praising God, who gave it to us," he was saying. "And that's just what I'd like your husband to support me on, Mrs. Mason. These days the holiday is less about the bounty the Lord has provided us, as our ancestors intended it to be, and more about entertainment and gluttony."

My mother and Teresa were scurrying around the kitchen, cooking, while doing their best to listen politely to the Reverend's opinions. For a few years now, he'd been on a campaign to get my father's support to turn Thanksgiving Day into a day of fasting, something folks in town used to do. And now here he was again, trying to win over the family and get at Daddy that way. But if there was one thing the people of Dogwood liked almost as much as God, it was food, and my family only humored the Reverend whenever he went into one of these lectures (while eating a plateful of my mama's cooking, no less).

I was past the point of humoring him. Saying a curt hello, I trudged over to the table and picked up a handful of biscuits, which were now even staler than the ones I'd had this morning. I handed one to Katie and we leaned against the wall, nibbling.

"You mark my words, Mrs. Mason, we can not afford to lose the sanctity of His laws and stop appreciating His blessings. Do you know what that kind of lawlessness has brought to the world outside of our blessed little town? Murder. Cruelty. Greed."

Absently I stared across the kitchen at my brother, who was sitting almost directly behind the Reverend. Noticing my sad and sour mood, Theo began to make faces for the sole purpose of annoying me.

First he made a fake sympathy face, knitting his eyebrows as if to say, "Aw, poor Glory. What's the matter?" Seeing my glare, he started laughing silently, in a real exaggerated way, which only made me madder. My mother and Teresa were too busy and distracted to pay attention, which only made Theo bolder. I clutched my biscuit in anger, my fingernails digging into the

~ 29

hard crust. Katie was studiously not looking at either one of us.

The Reverend had moved on to the subject of women and how it was our duty as keepers of the "domestic sphere" (which means the home) to encourage our men to be moral. "And the *children*," he said, throwing his hand out to indicate me. As if I were just a convenient example and not a real person with ears. "What are we teaching them when we reject the traditional ways? Just look at how lost and deviant they are becoming."

I didn't even know what the word *deviant* meant, but it sounded insulting. I threw my mama a quick glance. She gave me a look that said she was only humoring him. She didn't dare speak up for me—it would have been considered rude.

Reverend Clifton went on and on, saying things about "the children" that everyone knew were really aimed at me. Behind his back, Theo pointed at me, then waved his finger as if backing up the Reverend's point. Normally I would have just ignored him, but at that moment I felt rage fill me from my toenails to the tips of my hair. I could feel my face going beet red with the unfairness of it all.

Before I really knew what I was doing, I had cocked back the hand holding the stale biscuit.

The next second seemed to go in slow motion. The biscuit arced across the room, sailing across the table. I had time to see my mother's hands fly to her face in shock. And I had time to regret what I'd just done.

My aim was good. The biscuit hurtled toward Theo in a perfect straight line. But before it got there, Reverend Clifton leaned ever so slightly forward.

You could hear the *thunk* as the biscuit hit him. "Aouowww!" The Reverend's hand flew up in a flash to clutch his right temple. He exploded out of his seat, stunned, his chair toppling over with a clatter as he looked around for whatever had hit him.

"Glory!" Teresa gasped. The kitchen was suddenly dead silent; the Reverend watched in stunned disbelief as a decent-sized, round, and very stale biscuit bounced away across the kitchen floor. He looked at me, his mouth moving but with no words coming out, like a fish gasping for water. Then he looked back at the biscuit, then back at me. I wasn't angry anymore. I just felt stunned.

In my thirteen years I'd seen the Reverend pretty angry (and usually it was at me). But I'd never seen his face turn *purple.* Maybe it was partly from the biscuit hitting so hard. In any case, I felt Katie's hand slip into mine. I knew she wanted to run because Katie hated trouble more than anything, but she stood fast beside me. I had to hand it to her—that was pretty brave. Truth be told, I kind of wanted to run, too.

But something in the Reverend's purple face told me that getting out of this wasn't going to be as easy as running away.

CHAPTER
THREE

I spent Sunday in the main town garden. I'd been sentenced to a full week's work there—a record (and on *top* of my everyday chores). Mama wasn't speaking to me. I even had to work straight through Sunday worship, planting the winter crop of greens. And Daddy would have tanned my hide but for Mama telling him I was too old.

So instead of a whipping I'd had to go without any Thanksgiving dinner, and Daddy'd forbidden me from seeing Katie for a week. Which didn't make any sense, in my opinion, because Mama and Daddy were always saying Katie was a good influence on me, and now, when I needed a good influence most, I was stuck in the garden by myself.

"Glory!"

Scrunch. I sank my rake into the soil and craned my neck under my floppy straw hat, looking first up the hill—toward the church—then down. Out of the corner of my eye, I detected something moving just beyond the garden fence. Staring for a second, I finally made out Katie's face peering at me through the slats.

I swiped at the dirt on my face and grinned. "Katie! Whoo, am I glad to see you!"

Katie was wearing a big smile on her face and her chestnut hair in a bun. In her right hand she held a stack of cookies. In her left was a tin mug with a lid on top.

"Now hurry up before I get in trouble," she said, waving the hand with the cookies and pushing the mug through a slat in the wooden fence. I stole a quick look toward the church windows, trudged over, and took the cookies from her, tucking them into my right pocket. Then I pulled the lid off the mug and took a gulp. Hot chocolate. It was warm and thick and sweet.

"Thanks," I said, offering her back the mug for a sip. "How'd you get out of . . . ?" I nodded up toward the church to finish my sentence. There were at least a couple more hours until worship was over. Folks had just launched into "How Great Thou Art," and Reverend Clifton only ever used that when he was getting warmed up. Soon they'd be dancing and waving their hands in the air and shouting the Lord's praise, which was much better than the first half of church (which was listening to Scriptures).

"Mama and I told Daddy I wasn't feeling well." Katie's soft blue eyes danced—she looked like the cat who had swallowed the canary. Like she knew I'd be shocked. And I was, 'cause Katie never lied, and neither did her mother. "Mama was feeling sorry for you, so she baked those cookies special last night. But Glory," she said, her eyebrows knitting together thoughtfully, "she said to tell you she wants you to start trying to mind your folks and the Reverend. She's worried you're going to get yourself in a real mess one of these days."

I shrugged, chewing a big mouthful of cookie. Mrs. Johansen understood a lot of things about me, and so did Katie. And truly, I felt bad for what had happened—for embarrassing my family, and mostly for putting Katie in the middle of it. I even felt a little bad about the Reverend, although I thought that he was making a big deal out of something very little and that he'd deserved a biscuit in the head besides. Still, Katie and her mama didn't know what it was like being me. Sometimes it felt like if I didn't act up every once in a while, I'd just shrivel up and disappear. Either that or explode. And I didn't figure they could ever understand that.

"Aw, if I wasn't getting myself in trouble, how would we feed the town?" I joked, sweeping my arm out in front of my chest to indicate all the work I'd done today. "More greens than you could ever hope for." Three rows of spinach and three of kale lined the freshly tilled soil in front of me. And that was just from today. On Friday and Saturday, I'd helped to rake all the refuse off the unused part of the garden (the part that stayed bare all winter) and laid down mulch to protect the roots of the plants that would grow again next year. And tomorrow Mr. Lincoln, the chief gardener, and I were going to harvest a whole bunch of apples from the trees on the edge of town, then bury them on the far side of the garden to keep for winter baking.

"But your daddy . . ."

"Oh, please, don't let's start on my daddy," I said, tapping irritably at a chunk of manure on the tip of my boot. I hadn't fully forgiven my daddy for being so mean to me the other day, especially since he'd been even meaner after he found out about the biscuit-throwing. And I had no interest in talking about his rules and why it was so important for me to follow them. "Y'all take him way too seriously."

I expected Katie to protest, out of respect for Daddy, but she wasn't paying attention anymore. She was looking over my head, her eyes wide. I turned around just in time to see—who else?—my daddy, stomping the last few yards across the garden to where we were standing. Katie and I both stood up a little straighter. It was a reflex.

"Hi, Mr. Mason."

"Hi, Daddy, Katie was just—"

"Katie, shouldn't you be in bed? I heard you were feeling ill." Daddy loomed over us, his normally disheveled black hair combed back neatly so that only a few wisps peeked out from behind his ears. His big, rough hands slid back and forth along his belt fitfully. Daddy never was comfortable in Sunday clothes. I could tell with one look that he didn't for a minute believe that Katie was sick.

"She was just leaving," I said, turning and giving Katie a

look that said, "Scoot." I didn't need to. She was already waving and backing away.

"See you later, Glory; bye, Mr. Mason." She turned and hurried toward her house.

Now it was just me and my daddy standing there, but I didn't really feel like talking to him. And I didn't know what to say, anyway. So I just picked up my shovel and went back to work. Daddy just stood there for a second, clearing his throat.

"The Reverend told me you apologized to him, Glory."

"Mm-hmm," I said, sinking my shovel into the dirt. I tried to sound respectful but also like I wasn't interested.

"From the way he tells it, it wasn't the most sincere apology he's ever heard." I just kept digging until Daddy finally put his hand below my chin and made me look at him. His face was full of concern. "Would it hurt for you to tell him you're sorry and actually sound like you mean it?"

I shrugged and pulled my chin away. "Daddy, I just can't be sorry about the Reverend. I'm just not, and I can't say that I am. He's truly awful sometimes, the way he bosses everyone around. And he knows I didn't mean to hit him with that biscuit. It was an accident, but he won't let it go."

Daddy tilted his head and looked up at me from under his eyebrows. "You always think you're in the right, Glory. I know. But one day you'll find out you don't know as much as you think you do. And that's when you'll really learn what being a young lady is. With that biscuit stunt, you proved you're still just a child."

I swallowed. On his face was this look of worry mixed with sternness that made it seem like he could see right into my heart—into all the ornery thoughts tucked away there, crowding the guilty and sorry thoughts into a corner. Ornery thoughts like, *Maybe I don't want to be a young lady.* All I said was, "Yes, sir."

After staring into me for a moment longer, his face softened again. "I know it's hard not to question things," he said, reaching out and ruffling up the top of my hair. "Maybe it's my fault for encouraging you so long. Still, your judgment has to catch up with your strong will eventually.

"You remind me of myself when I was young," he went on. "Only you're even more stubborn." He smiled. "I keep waiting for you to put the stubbornness aside because when you do, I think you'll be a fine woman."

I smiled back at him. I was thrilled to have this kind of talk with him again and thrilled that he saw a good future for me. But at the same time I just didn't see how I could change the way I felt. I wanted to make Daddy happy, but how could I be anything but me?

"Now get back to work," he said, the left side of his mouth tilting up. "I've got business to attend to downhill."

He turned away, and I watched him get smaller and smaller as he trudged down toward the valley. I shoved one hand in the pocket of my coveralls to absentmindedly finger what was left of my cookies, feeling happy we were made up. I wondered if that was why he'd come out in the first place. But then, watching him walk on down the hill, I realized that of course there must be a shipment coming in. That was the only thing important enough to cut into church.

Shipments rarely came to Dogwood, and they always came in trucks. *That* was exciting enough 'cause those trucks were the only automobiles that ever came anywhere near town and the men driving them were the only strangers. But then, *also,* there were the things they brought—mostly boring supplies like coal and whatnot, but sometimes there were extras—like secondhand clothes, fabric, paint, canned goods, even fresh fruit—that Daddy and Mr. Johansen would distribute when they saw fit.

And then, every so often, there came the things we weren't supposed to know about—the big canvas sacks, the mysterious crates that stayed in the shed forever. Whenever I bugged Daddy about it long enough, he'd say it was stuff for protecting the town should Uncle Sam ever try to take our lifestyle away from us. Uncle Sam is what Daddy calls the world outside of Dogwood. And I guess it also means the people in charge out there, like the government.

They'd carry the big loads into the shed, and what happened after that was a mystery, because like I mentioned, once that stuff went in, most people never saw it again. The place was tightly locked up, and the only people allowed to enter were a few of the men.

A few minutes after he had gone down the hill, a truck rumbled up to meet my daddy, sure enough. It was a big, muddy green thing with a slat rail around the trailer bed. Through the slats I could see mounds of sacks and crates, covered by blue canvas.

After talking to Daddy for a minute or two, the driver got back in the truck and backed it up close to the shed doors. I squinted at them as together they unloaded sack after sack of supplies. They disappeared inside for several minutes.

When they came out, the men slammed the shed door shut. They talked for a few seconds more, their heads hunched together. Then the stranger and his truck went off down the mountain. Daddy watched him go, his hands on his belt and his head tilted to one side. He then turned and headed back up toward the church. As he passed the garden, *my* garden (as I'd come to think of it from all the being in trouble), he looked serious and thoughtful—like his eyes were focused on something miles and miles away. But when he noticed me standing there watching him, he gave me a little grin and a wave as he kept on up the hill.

After he'd gone, I started raking again. *Scrunch ting. Scrunch ting.* I was too exhausted to think very hard, but something was gnawing at me. Something I couldn't quite put my finger on.

Scrunch ting. I dragged myself to the top of the garden to pick up a bunch of kale, then turned around, walked back, and bent down, dropping the kale's roots into the hole I'd made and patting the black soil all around it until it felt solid. When were we going to eat all these greens, anyway? If Mama made that pork stew with kale again, that would be it. I wouldn't eat a bite. And if Theo . . .

Then it hit me. The shed door.

Daddy hadn't locked it.

The door made such an awful creaking noise that for a minute I was sure someone would hear. I took a few fast steps backward so I could see the church . . . but there was nothing. Except lots of singing. I silently thanked God that I didn't have to be there. *It's not anything personal, God,* I thought. It was just that I didn't like standing in a stuffy old room all day and then dancing around singing about the Lord.

I padded back over to the big shed door, which had opened just far enough for a skinny girl-body like mine to squeeze through. I pressed my face toward the opening, my right cheek resting against the rough wood.

Of course, the conversation my daddy and I had just had rang through my head. I felt guilty. But the thing was, he *had* always encouraged me to think for myself. And it wasn't like I could just stop all of a sudden. And if I was supposed to be an adult, then shouldn't I know about these things? And it wasn't like anybody was going to find out. I needed to know what was in the shed. I just needed to.

The air drifting out to me was cool and musty. It smelled like old hay and canvas and something else. I took one last look around and slid inside.

The room was shadowy, but not dark. Sunlight filtered in through seams in the door, and I noticed a loose slat in the wall. It hung diagonally, making a skinny, triangle-shaped strip of light along the dirt floor. As my eyes got accustomed to the shadows, I let my hands run over the curious objects in the room. There were three whole cases of canned fruit and a case of wine, which I knew must be for church, stacked up in one corner. There were drums of oil and a few bolts of fabric, piles of long, red candles all tied up together in rows, and sacks of coffee and coal. Along the back wall there were four giant crates covered with canvas and topped with square planks of wood. Seeing those crates sent a chill down my spine. I knew they were the supplies that never came out.

I tiptoed over to them slowly, as if whatever was inside might come to life and attack me if I made too much noise. One of the strips of sunlight coming from the door fell across the crate on the far left, and that's the one I finally settled on. I stood with my toes touching the wood, my breathing coming short all of a sudden. If someone else were in the same room, would they be able to hear my heart beat? It felt that loud. What would I find in here?

Slowly I lifted the wooden lid of the crate and rested it against the wall. I stared down at the canvas, then put my hand on top of it. Whatever was underneath felt cool and solid, like metal. I took a deep breath and grasped the edge of the canvas in my hand.

That's when I saw it. At eye level, on a shelf above the crate. A radio.

I'd never seen one in real life, but I knew what it was from Mrs. Johansen's stories. I instantly forgot about the canvas and carefully, carefully pulled the radio down from the shelf. I gently set my treasure down on the edge of the crate and studied it. On the top there were two switches and a dial. One switch said On/Off. Another said AM/FM. The dial didn't say anything. On the side was a knob that said volume.

My heart was pounding double time now, but this time it was from a happy kind of excitement. Ever since I could remember, radios had been forbidden in Dogwood. Daddy always said allowing them in would bring loose morals into our lives. I had always wondered what it was about a radio that could be so sinful. Well, now I would find out.

Sending a silent prayer up to God, promising that I would keep my good morals no matter what I heard on the radio, I flicked the on-off switch. The noise that came out was so loud that I must have jumped about twenty feet in the air. Quickly I fumbled for the volume knob on the side and turned it all the way down. Then I stood very still and listened for a sign that someone uphill had heard. Nothing. I couldn't even hear the noises from the church anymore. I knew worship couldn't be over yet, but I'd have to head up to the garden soon to be on the safe side.

I turned back to the radio and turned the volume up ever so slightly. There was lots of fuzzy noise and then a man's voice, talking about God. I fiddled with the dial on top, which made the sounds change from one thing to another, from the man's voice, to fuzz, to another voice, to fuzz again. And then, suddenly, there was music.

A woman was singing the same words over and over—about a boy who made her feel like she was spinning around in a hurricane. Her voice was soulful and deep and soft at the same time, and these other women were singing in the background, and there were these incredible beats.

Strange, huge happiness took over my entire body. I held the sides of the radio and laughed because I didn't know what else to do. I couldn't keep my body from moving to the music, either, and pretty soon I was rocking back and forth, the radio bouncing on the edge of the crate with every move I made. Keeping my voice low, I sang along with the words I could pick up.

It wasn't that I hadn't heard music before. I'd heard plenty of spirituals and folk songs passed down through generations of my kinfolk. Before he died, my uncle Cecil used to play "Down in the Meadow" on a silver harmonica he had, and I loved it so much that if I was in the right frame of mind, it could make me cry.

But I'd never heard anything like this.

Minutes must have gone by as one song turned into another. Then another. And each song moved fast and had all sorts of instruments in the background, and I just had to move. And I kind of forgot about everything else.

I guess that's why I didn't hear the shed door creak as it opened all the way. But I saw the strip of sunlight from the door widen into a giant rectangle in front of me. I watched my shadow rise crookedly from the floor, along the crate in front of me, up the wall. And then I saw another shadow. A big, man's shadow.

I whirled around, and suddenly my heart felt like it was dropping right out the bottom of my feet and floating up and away to somewhere just above the roof. Because there was my daddy, his frame filling up the doorway—and his eyes were blacker than murder.

CHAPTER
FOUR

"OH COME LET US ADOOOORE HIIIIIM! CHRIIIIIIST THE LOOOOORD!"

Katie and I triumphantly finished the chorus of our favorite hymn, gasping for breath and laughing. Even Theo looked amused, not annoyed and superior the way he most often did. There's nothing like being out in the woods for an excuse to sing at the top of your lungs.

It was the day before Christmas Eve—the last and best time before winter would settle in and make life in Dogwood cold and dull. The forest was a white and sparkling version of itself in the summertime—instead of green leaves and sunlight and shadows there were crystal-covered trees, streams frozen in ripples, giant rocks dripping icicles. Theo, Katie, and I trudged along, Theo and I dragging our newly chopped Christmas tree behind us through the knee-deep snow, proud as Indian warriors returned from the hunt.

Even though it was cold, our cheeks were red and moist from the exercise. I tugged my wool cap back from my forehead, brushing some of my sweat-sticky hair out of my eyes with a mitten.

"Hey, Theo, do you think this tree is bigger than last year's?" I looked up at my brother hopefully.

Theo glanced back at the tree real serious for a second, like he was sizing it up. "Well, Glory, I can't say for sure if it's bigger or not, but it sure is the prettiest Christmas tree I ever saw."

"Me too," Katie added, even though I knew Mr. Johansen had brought home a beauty the week before. "You both did a fine job. Your daddy's going to be real proud, Glory."

I couldn't quite carry off the smile I tried to give her. She was humoring me, I knew. They both were. Partly because it was Christmas, and everybody in Dogwood's extra nice to each other that time of year. And partly because Katie, and even Theo, had been nicer than usual lately, trying to make me feel better. The truth was, things had changed between Daddy and me since the day of the radio.

When Daddy had found me in the shed, he hadn't yelled or anything like that. Instead he'd just been really quiet. We'd walked home together, with me stealing a glance at his face now and then, but it was like he didn't even notice me. And somehow that was scarier than getting yelled at or punished.

For the past few weeks he'd treated me like a stranger—and not just in public. Even when we were alone, he'd stopped laughing at my jokes or ruffling my hair. It wasn't that he wasn't speaking to me, it was just that he was speaking to me like I was someone else. Whenever I tried to start a conversation with him, he'd be polite, but he wouldn't argue with me like he used to or encourage me to think about things in this or that way.

He hadn't told anyone what had happened that day, even my mama—I think he was scared I'd get in too much trouble for it with the town folk—but my family must've noticed how he was acting. I thought he must have decided that I was beyond help, beyond hope. Katie said maybe he thought that if he started treating me like an adult, I'd start acting like one. But figuring on that didn't stop it from hurting my feelings. And I knew it wouldn't stop me from being rambunctious. I just couldn't help it.

Anyhow, I *was* proud of this tree. Mama had actually allowed me to cut it down this year, with Theo's help. And I thought I had done a fine job of picking it out *and* handling the ax. I couldn't wait to walk through our front door and show it off to everyone. Teresa and Mama would exclaim about how it was the best tree we'd ever had, like they did every year, and we'd set about putting it up and decorating it right away.

I was not going to let Daddy get me down. In Dogwood, Christmas is probably the most important day of the year, and even though you'd think it would be all about Jesus' birthday and being holy and such, it's also a lot about singing and being merry and exchanging presents and having parties and having the perfect tree and eating. And who wouldn't be excited about that?

There was a whole lot to do before tomorrow, which was the night of my folks' big Christmas Eve party. I'd already helped Mama scrub everything in the house from top to bottom while Teresa worked on the cakes and pies and cookies, which I was no good at. We'd washed the walls with vinegar and water and cleaned the curtains, putting them out on stretchers to dry. Once the house was spic-and-span, we'd trimmed every little nook and corner we could find with the holly branches and pinecones Katie and I'd gathered from the woods. Theo had chopped loads of extra wood to keep the fireplace and the woodstove burning all night long.

And Daddy . . . well, he was mostly too busy to help with the decorating. He had put in his two cents on my going to chop down the tree, though—saying it was boy's work and not fitting for a young lady. But Mama had stepped in for me. And it wasn't at all like Mama to speak up against Daddy's wishes. I guess she must've felt sorry for me, on account of how things had been between me and him lately.

Maybe, I thought, when Daddy saw the tree, he'd realize I could do things just as well as a boy. Maybe it would help him see, just a little bit, that I wasn't meant to be a dainty young lady like he wanted. Maybe.

"Ooh, there's mistletoe!" Katie hollered, veering off our path to pluck the stems with their white berries from a nearby bush. "You know, Glory, you're not allowed to whup Thomas with a stick if he tries to kiss you *under the mistletoe.*"

"Well, then, I'll stay far away from it," I answered.

Katie and Theo looked at each other and shrugged. That really got my goat. It was a shrug that said everyone knew that no matter how I argued against it, me and Thomas Johansen would of course be married someday. Just because we were the same age and he liked me, and in Dogwood that was as good as being engaged. Which made me mad because I wasn't interested in getting married, and especially not to Thomas—who got all googly-eyed every time he saw me, which was every blessed day—or to any other boy in Dogwood, for that matter. If I ever did get married, it was going to be to a sophisticated, modern boy from Boston or someplace like that. A boy version of Mrs. Johansen, who would come to town and build me a sophisticated house with contraptions in it and sometimes take me away on trips to Lord knew where, whether the town said I was allowed to go or not.

"Well," Katie said with a sigh, "there's got to be *some* romance on Christmas. You're going to get under the mistletoe with Lizzie, aren't you, Theo?"

Theo's cheeks went red, and he nervously shifted his grip on the tree. "Whadda you mean?"

"Well, you know she'll be disappointed if you don't." Katie smiled her sweetest, most flattering smile, her blue eyes practically glowing.

"Really?" Theo asked, sounding younger than his fifteen

years for a moment. I rolled my eyes. Well, of course Lizzie Taylor liked my brother. It was either him or the Whites' big-nosed son, who was almost as homely as his dad.

Katie continued to weave along behind us, keeping an eye on the underbrush and small trees. Every once in a while she bent down to pick up a pinecone or holly branch and put it in her gathering sack, saving up for decorations to bring home to her mama for their own tree. Theo, too, ducked now and then to pick up something or other and hand it back to Katie.

"Well, I'm going to turn off here," Katie said as we reached the edge of town. "I'll be over right after dinner. You sure it's all right with your mama if I spend the night?"

"Of course," I said.

"Good. Well, bye." Katie wagged a mitten in our direction and turned on her boot heels.

"See you tonight," Theo and I said in unison as she threaded her way across the snow, leaving deep footprints dotted behind her.

Watching her go, I sighed at the prospect of all the work ahead of us tonight. Theo interrupted my thoughts.

"You know, Glory, you sure were smart to choose that girl for a best friend."

For a moment I looked at Theo slant-eyed, wondering if he was now sweet on Katie instead of Lizzie. That would be a disaster. But the expression he wore reassured me. It was the same expression everyone wore when they talked about Katie. I don't know if it was her good manners, or her good looks, or her good heart, or the combination of all three, but she always brought out the best, warmest feelings in people. Including my brother. *And* including me.

"Well, she's the only girl I know near my age, so I didn't have a choice, did I?" I said, a little jealous that nobody felt that way about me.

But I was proud all the same.

Back home, everyone was in a tizzy except for baby Marie, who was sleeping soundly on the rug by the hearth.

Theo and I trudged in through the back door, loudly kicking off our boots and yanking off our mittens, hats, and scarves, hanging them by the stove to dry. The smells that greeted us— cinnamon, burning wood, stewed apples, and that smell of a cozy room on a cold day—were heavenly.

Teresa was standing over a big pot of dumplings, stirring with a wooden spoon, steam drifting up and condensing on her face. Mama was poised with a tray of gingerbread in her hand, about to place it up on the warming shelf above the oven. Tendrils of her hair were pasted to her face, and there was a dot of flour on her chin, standing out against her olive skin. Upon seeing us enter, they both put down what they were doing and ran to the back door.

"Oh, it's wonderful!" Teresa declared, just the way I knew she would. I loved Teresa, but you could never call her a surprising person.

"It certainly is a fine-looking tree," Mama added. "Good job, Glory, Theo."

Just then Daddy came in through the same door, carrying a stack of wood in his arms. I sucked in my breath, waiting for him to look at the tree. At the very least, he'd have to say a nice word or two about it.

He dropped the wood in its place by the stone hearth. "Smells mighty good in here, girls," he said, running a hand along Teresa's silky pigtail, then giving Mama a squeeze. He cast a quick look down at the tree, then at me. "Glory, go get yourself cleaned up and come help your mother and sister."

With that, he turned around and headed back outside, probably to tend to the usual town affairs.

I bit my lip. *Never mind,* I told myself, *never mind.* I turned toward the stairs so that no one would see the hurt written all over my face. But as I did, Mama grabbed my hand and turned me back around. She wet the tip of her pinky with her tongue and swiped at the hair hanging over my forehead, smoothing it back.

"It's a wonderful tree, Glory," she whispered. Then she patted my bottom and went back to her baking.

By the time we got the tree up, it was dusk. Usually things

calmed down this time of day because there wasn't much light to see by, but tonight Mama had every lamp going. Teresa draped the popcorn strings she'd made around the tree, and all of us set about trimming the branches with gingerbread and candles and a corn-husk angel at the top.

Sometimes I longed for electric lights like Mrs. Johansen talked about having in the outside world. But at Christmastime, I figured nothing could beat the lamps and the candles and the fireplace bathing the house in a warm orange glow—especially when the tree was all lit up, too. The heat from the fire made the pine needles smell extra good, and it put us all in the happiest mood. By the time Katie arrived, we were singing carols and carrying on like it was already Christmas Day and not two days before.

Katie and I settled right into work, with me on the couch and Katie in my mama's rocking chair, two huge spools of spun wool between us. For the past three and a half weeks we'd been slaving over mittens, hats, and scarves to give to all the kids in Dogwood as Christmas presents, and tonight we were going to be up until all hours finishing them. It had been Katie's idea, and I'd jumped at the chance to do something so artful. But now it was just getting to be plain tedious and nerve-racking.

Lord knew I didn't have the patience for this, though I tried to follow Katie's example as she sat serenely rocking in the chair next to me. Maybe if I were in the rocking chair, I'd feel better, I thought. Or maybe I had the bad wool and Katie had wool that was easier to knit. Or maybe my needles just weren't working right. Certainly Katie's pile was growing much faster than mine and looked ten times better. One of my mittens even had two thumbs instead of one.

I was just starting to really stew when Katie threw another perfect hat on her pile. The rest of the household had gone to bed, and the fire was getting dim and low. Roused out of my silent impatience and noticing the chill in the room, I pulled my afghan tighter around my legs.

"Do you ever wonder how they know when Jesus' birthday really is?" I asked.

Katie looked over at me, her forehead wrinkled, her hands already at work on a new row of knitting.

"I mean," I continued, "don't you think they just picked a day on a guess? Because I really don't know how they could know for sure what day He was born, especially with the whole B.C.–A.D. thing and all."

Katie's look of confusion turned into a sweet smile. "Oh, Glory, I don't know. I don't think it matters, do you?"

"Well, yes, I do think it matters." Now I had completely put down my knitting, glad for the distraction of a conversation. "Because it gets my goat that the Reverend and everyone would say that this day is definitely Christ's birthday when it may not be at all."

Katie opened her mouth to speak, but I continued. "I mean, doesn't it make you wonder what else they don't know and tell us they do? Like how certain things are sinful and certain things aren't, and what a woman's place is and how we have to be young ladies and all? You know, things like that?" I guess I'd been stewing about more than just mittens.

My best friend looked thoughtful, like she usually did when you brought up questions that some people would just be mad at you for asking. Finally she spoke. "Well, I think it's probably true that the old folks in town aren't always right about everything. But the way I see it, they're trying their best. And I think we're lucky. You know, most places they don't look out for each other like they do here. That's what my mama says. I guess if they're wrong about some of the details, that's all right with me, as long as they get the big things right."

For some reason, that just made me madder. "Yeah, but what about big things like getting to be whoever you want, even if you're a girl? And getting to go where you want, like if we wanted to go to Boston for real?"

Katie leaned over and squeezed my hand, looking somehow as wise as an old lady instead of a girl my age. "Oh, Glory, you're so smart and brave. I think they have those rules 'cause most of us couldn't handle that stuff—I mean, going so far away—but I bet *you* could. You could take the world by storm, Glory Bee Mason. My mama says so, too.

"But you know," she added, her serious blue eyes looking deeply into mine, "we do get to be who we are here. I do because it's easy for me to fit in. And you do because you're a fighter. It's something that makes me proud of you."

"You're proud I'm a troublemaker?" I snorted, but I hung on what she'd say next.

"I'm proud you stand up for yourself. It's one of my favorite things about you."

Katie turned back to her knitting with a shrug, as if she hadn't just given me the biggest compliment of my life. And complimented me on the very thing that everybody else was always criticizing me for.

"Just three more to go." She sighed, her mind already somewhere else as she turned back to her knitting.

I didn't say anything. I was speechless.

As we lay in bed that night, the moon shining through my gauzy white curtains and across the bed that Katie and I were sharing, I thought about God. I thought about how the Reverend was always saying God didn't like my ornery ways and that if I didn't repent, I'd never get into heaven. And I thought about what Katie had said, and how the two just didn't seem to match up.

Me and God had been having a rocky relationship lately, and it made me feel lonely sometimes. Lots of times I felt mad that God would want me to be something other than what I was, and then every once in a while I felt sorry for not being what I was supposed to be. But maybe the Reverend was wrong. If Katie wanted me to be myself, maybe God did, too.

And tonight, after thinking about the good of Him and the bad of Him and trying to make it all add up in my head, I felt only one thing before I drifted off to sleep, and that was thankfulness. For Christmas and for home and for being alive. And especially for Katie.

CHAPTER
FIVE

The only person in town who didn't show up at our annual Christmas party was Reverend Clifton. Not that it was any surprise. He'd never come—not in the seven years that we'd been having it. It was one of the few times when Daddy and the rest of the town went against Reverend Clifton, since no one else thought he was right when he said parties were no way to celebrate the Lord's birth. He said he would rather commune quietly in his home with God, but last year when Katie and I got bored and sneaked over to his house to see what he meant by "communing," we saw it was basically lying on his sofa, snoring. This year we figured he was probably doing the same thing. Which was maybe why my daddy didn't feel bad about having the party.

I'd been trying to help Teresa in the kitchen all afternoon, but she'd finally shooed me out when I'd almost set the black walnut cake on fire, and since Mama and Daddy were greeting the guests, I could just sit with Katie and admire the festivities, which suited me fine.

Katie and I had parked ourselves up on the stairs, which

looked down on the foyer but were hidden from the front door by a thick banister. We sat there for at least an hour, watching all the guests come in bringing goodies and kissing each other and smiling. For some people we jumped up to say hello, and for some people we just stayed put.

"Why, don't you look nice, Dr. Venable, Jane," Mama said as Katie and I watched through the banister posts. Mama's hair cascaded down her neck in soft brown curls, and she was wearing the high-collared dress that Mrs. Johansen had made her as a Christmas present years ago. Daddy stood like a pillar beside her, looking—like always—too big for the room he was standing in as he greeted the doctor and his wife, then Mr. and Mrs. White.

I rolled my eyes at Katie and gestured like I was smoking a pipe. She giggled as we leaned back into the shadows. We watched in silence as Mama ushered them toward the cider and the chicken and dumplings.

I was restless. Despite everything—the tantalizing smells of supper and the dazzle of everyone dressed up in their finest—I was feeling a bit let down by this year's party. The littler youngsters were running around playing games, and the older ones were huddled in corners telling secrets, but for me, none of that seemed inviting. My eyes kept drifting to Daddy, who was still treating me like a stranger. The longer I sat there, the more I felt the unfairness of it all. He'd taught me to ask questions. How could he expect me to just snuff out my curiosity the way you snuff a candle?

"Why don't we get out of here?" I suggested to Katie.

"And do what?" she asked dubiously.

"Well, I dunno." I sighed. "Um, we could go spy on the Reverend, or . . ."

The idea came to me so suddenly that it almost felt like it couldn't have come from my very own brain.

"There *is* something," I said, my stomach getting hot with fear and nervousness but also with excitement, "but you may not want to do it."

Katie got a mock-defensive look in her eyes. "Oh, you're not the only daring girl in this town, Glory Mason. I'll do it. You just lead the way."

The town was beautiful and very hushed. The houses, usually so angular and visible against the fields, seemed to blend into the slopes of the nearby mountains, their roofs curved and softened under layers of pure white snow.

The shed door was locked, like I'd expected. I set down the plate of ham and greens and stewed apples I was carrying, which I'd told Teresa I was bringing to the Reverend (as an excuse for us leaving), and felt my way around the corner, into the shadows on the dark side of the building. Taking my left mitten off with my teeth, I slid my cold fingers along the boards and quickly found the board I'd noticed the day of the radio. The one that was loose.

"Here," I whispered, though nobody could have possibly heard us since they were all across town.

"Glory—are you sure?" Katie asked me, wide-eyed.

I stared back at her, my eyebrows raised in a dare.

With a sigh, Katie came quickly around the side of the shed and stood beside me as I pulled at the board to loosen it more. When the opening was wide enough, she slipped inside, with me close at her heels.

Drinking spirits was supposed to be a terrible sin, according to the Reverend and Daddy and all the rest of the grown-ups. And here I was, making Katie commit a sin right along with me. But when I really thought about it, the idea that drinking spirits was sinful just seemed like a bunch of hooey to me. After all, Jesus drank wine—and made all his apostles drink it, too. Not to mention that every grown-up in town drank it at mass every Sunday, even though they only drank a drop. And even on top of that, Mrs. Johansen had told me once about how her brothers got drunk on moonshine one time, and she'd laughed the whole way through the story—talking about how silly they'd acted and how they couldn't say their words properly.

How could something that was perfectly okay in little amounts, and so funny to boot, be evil?

Maybe I was just making excuses to myself because I was so

all-fired curious to try it out. I had no idea what being drunk could possibly feel like . . . and I really wanted to know. And, well, it was Christmas Eve, and so far I hadn't had any fun at all.

Using one of my feet, I shoved the wooden slat closed behind us. It was pitch-dark in the shed, but warmer because we were now out of the wind. I pulled out the candle I'd tucked into my coat and Katie pulled out the coal she'd been keeping warmed in a covered tin mug. After a few seconds, the candle was lit and the room was very dimly aglow.

It took me no time at all to locate the wine, because I remembered exactly where it had been. I carried a bottle back to where Katie was sitting cross-legged, pulling off her hat and scarf.

Seeing the bottle, she looked up at me from the cupped hands she'd been warming with her breath. "Glory, are you sure you want to do this?" she asked again.

"Sure as sure can be," I replied. "You haven't changed your mind, have you?" I unscrewed the bottle top and held the bottle out for her to take a whiff.

"Ick." She wrinkled her whole face in disgust. I pulled the bottle back to the tip of my own nose. It did smell awful. Like old dirty socks and sour grapes.

Katie and I looked at each other, and I truly expected her to back out right then and there. And I wouldn't have blamed her for it, either. There was the smell. And then I was already in so much trouble all the time that I didn't have much to lose, but

Katie . . . she was practically a saint in the town's eyes, and I knew the only reason she was even here was for my sake.

"Give me that," she said suddenly, trying to look brave but really looking nervous as all creation as she wrestled the bottle from my hands. I almost didn't want to give it up. I felt suddenly bad for dragging her along on this adventure.

She stared down at the bottle's mouth. "Well, here goes," she said with a sigh. And without another thought, she held her nose, tilted back her head, and took a huge swig. A shudder shook her whole body. Still keeping her eyes squeezed tightly shut, she held the bottle out to me.

I was impressed. And I figured we might as well plunge ahead now. I pulled the bottle up to my lips quick as a flash and drank two gulps, just wanting to get it over with. By the time I brought the bottle back down to my lap, the taste had settled in.

Katie looked the way I felt—disgusted. I held my breath, on the chance that it would make the wine take effect faster, and waited to feel something. But nothing happened. Not at first. Except that my cheeks felt kind of warm and I felt a bit ill.

I held my nose and threw back another gulp.

"Glory!" Katie squeaked.

"Well, nothing's happening," I said. "I want to make sure we drink enough to get it right."

Looking thoughtful, Katie took the bottle from me and did

the same. It was a very unpleasant few minutes, tastebud-wise. I wondered if God had made wine taste so bad on purpose, so people wouldn't commit the sin of drinking too much of it.

Within minutes we'd emptied half the bottle. We lounged back against the legs of a battered old couch and just stared at the light of the candle for a while.

Slowly, everything seemed to take on a glow, and I wondered if this was what getting drunk felt like. Instead of feeling cold and dark and lonely, the shed seemed to me the coziest, nicest place. The candlelight felt extra warm on my face, and my head was swimming with good thoughts. I even felt friendly toward Reverend Clifton and toyed with the idea of bringing him that plate of food after all. *See?* I told myself. *Being drunk isn't sinful at all. Why, it's gentle and . . . and nice.*

"What're your New Year's resolutions going to be?" Katie asked after a while.

"Oh, I haven't thought on that yet," I said dreamily, looking at the shadows dancing along the wooden walls. It seemed like we'd been sitting here forever.

"Well, I've been thinking on mine, and you know that talk we had the other night? I think you're right. I think we need to expand our lives, even if it's scary," Katie said, staring at the tiny flame in front of us.

I wondered vaguely what she meant by that. I felt too good to really care all that much.

Katie tilted back her head. "I think we should promise each other to get out of this town and go to Boston someday."

Whoa. I sat straight up.

"I mean, maybe not for good," she continued, "but at least for a trip. To see my mama's family there and just, well, just to *see* it. No matter what the Reverend or anyone else says."

I let out the breath I'd been unconsciously holding. Of all the times Katie and I had talked about Boston, and dreamed about Boston, and longed to see Boston, Katie had never agreed to go there with me. Now she was offering, without me even having to bug her, and I knew that she meant it. And even with all my big talk, I wouldn't want to go for good, either. So a trip to Boston, even for just a little while, was about the best thing I could ever imagine.

"Katherine Ruth Johansen," I said, taking her hand in a flimsy, wine-weakened shake. "That would be just fine by me."

I lifted the bottle. "I, Glory Bee Mason, um . . . promise to get the heck out of this . . . this . . . town someday and go to Boston. And ride in a car. With my friend. Katie." It occurred to me that it was getting harder to think of the words that went into making a sentence.

Katie grinned and put her hand over mine. "Me too."

The weight of her hand tilted the bottle and made it splash all over my coat. "Oh!" I cried.

Katie snorted, clutching her hand to her stomach. The snort

made me laugh, and pretty soon we were both almost rolling on the dirt floor. I laughed so hard, my eyes filled up with tears.

"I feel light, mmm, light as a feather," I said, leaning over and hugging Katie. Katie nodded enthusiastically, her head lolling up and down lazily, and then she took another big gulp. "You know, you're my bes' friend in the whole world," I said, giving her a kiss on the cheek.

"You know what I feel like doin'?" Katie breathed. "I feel like goin' down to the lake."

"Right now?" I asked, squinting at her.

"Yeah. Why not? I bet it's so beautiful right now, I bet it's all silver with ice."

"It's freezing out," I complained. I didn't want to leave our cozy nest.

"But I feel sooo warm," she said. "I don't think anything could make me feel cold. Come on. Let's go. It'll be fun."

I looked at the bottle, which was now lying almost empty on the floor.

"Well, I suppose we have nothin' better t' do," I admitted.

We both stood up, holding on to each other for balance. I felt like my brain was spinning in circles.

"Okay, less go," I murmured, picking my hat up off the floor. I blew out our candle, and then out through the loose slat we crawled—into the cold winter air with no scarves, no mittens, and with Katie only wearing her dressy brocade slippers. I hadn't bothered to pick up the bottle or tidy up the shed, but it didn't really seem all that important now. We turned left and swung in a wide arc around my house. Inside, everyone was singing "Oh, Come, All Ye Faithful." Mrs. White had a shrill voice that rang out above everyone else's, and for some reason, hearing it struck me as the funniest thing I'd ever heard and I had to put my hand over my mouth to hold my giggles in. Katie started giggling, too, and clutched my arm as she pulled me down the hill and onto the shadowy path that led to the lake.

By the time we were halfway down the path, I'd calmed down. And it was a good thing because I would've been too distracted to see that first glimpse of the lake, which took my breath away. A thin dusting of snow stood on the surface, and a small wind was blowing the loose flakes around so that it looked almost like ghosts swirling in the air. The trees looked black all around us, with their shadows making dark slashes across the smooth white ground. It was actually a little bit spooky.

"Whoa. It sure is beautiful," Katie said, tightening her arm around mine. I noticed she looked so, so pretty out under the bright moon. Big pink circles stood out on her cheeks, and her long eyelashes fluttered to keep out the swirling snow. I wondered if I looked that pretty, too, and then decided I definitely did not.

Katie smiled at me, then let go of my arm and ran the rest of the way to the lake. She stopped just at the edge and turned back to motion me forward. Before I could get halfway there, though, she'd already taken a few careful steps onto the ice.

"Hey, wait, Katie," I called. But she was ignoring me. As she moved farther and farther onto the lake, her steps gained confidence, and pretty soon she was probably about twenty feet out from the shore. She turned and looked at me.

"And now," she slurred, slipping and setting herself upright again, "I'm going to perform my favorite ballet scene, from *Swan Lake*." We knew all about ballet from Mrs. Johansen. She'd even taken ballet lessons when she was a little girl. Her favorite was *Swan Lake,* so of course it was Katie's and my favorite, too.

Katie started spinning around on the ice, faster and faster, kicking up a whirl of snow dust in her wake.

"Katie, be careful," I called from the edge. "You know, the lake hasn't been frozen all that—"

Wham! Before I could finish my sentence, she toppled off balance, landing with a thud on her back. My heart caught in my chest.

"Katie!" I cried from the edge, but she didn't move.

"Katie?" I touched a toe to the ice to test it, then rested my whole foot. My head was still spinning.

"Katie?" I took another step toward her, my voice cracking. Soon I was only a couple of feet away from her.

Suddenly she sat up and held her arms straight above her, ballet-style. "Laaa . . ." she sang, rising to her feet, pretending to be graceful.

"You faker!" I picked up two handfuls of snow and hurled them at her as she bowed and smiled. She ducked, laughing, and covered her head with her arms.

"You're an awful ballerina!" I called, and picked up another lump of snow, hurling it at her with double force. She dodged, squealing, "No!" and tried to get out of range. But I wasn't going to let her get away. I scooped up another handful, this time patting it into a ball for maximum impact. Cocking back my elbow, I took aim and slung it at her as hard as I could. It hit the mark, right on her forehead, and Katie stumbled backward, gasping with laughter.

Crack.

Katie and I locked eyes. Hers were wide with fear. The ice . . .

Crack.

There was a sound of water gurgling and then a ripping, splashing sound that tore right through my body, making my heart leap and pulling a scream out of my throat without me even willing it.

"Katie!"

But Katie had vanished from view. Forgetting the thinness of the ice, I ran toward the spot where she'd been standing and pulled up short. There was now only a jagged hole where she had been.

"Katie!" I screamed again. Tears burst from my eyes. I'd heard of people falling through the ice. I knew how deadly it could be. Quickly I lay down to spread my weight out on the frozen surface and reached an arm into the icy water.

Nothing. The water was so cold that after a few seconds I couldn't feel my arm anymore. I sucked in my breath and plunged my other arm forward over my head, fanning both of them under the water. My teeth started chattering uncontrollably. "Katie! Katie! Please, please, please!"

Nothing again. I just kept groping around in the black water, not knowing what else to do. "Help!" I screamed, even though I knew we were too far from town for anyone to hear.

Suddenly my hand brushed against something big and soft. I yanked with all the strength I could muster, and Katie's head bobbed to the surface. *Thank you, God.* Her face was white as milk and her eyes were closed, but she was there. I pulled again so that her head and chest were resting on the ice, but no sooner had I done it than the ice cracked under the weight and she slipped into the water again.

"Katie, wake up!" I screamed. "Somebody help!"

I tried three more times to drag her out of the water, but every time the ice cracked beneath her. There was no way I could do this alone. I had to get help.

"Okay, Katie," I said, pulling her arms up onto the ice and resting her chin against a jagged ridge. "I'll be right back, okay? Please wait for me. Please don't die, okay?" My voice cracked into a groan on these last words.

Slowly, carefully, I crawled backward off the ice, watching Katie the whole way to make sure she stayed on the surface. But the instant I felt solid earth beneath my feet, I jumped up and broke into a run, never looking back.

I sprinted up the long, twisting trail back to town. The snow shifting beneath me made it hard to keep my balance as I criss-crossed back and forth, breaking through frozen branches and underbrush, my breath puffing out behind me. It seemed like a hundred years went by before I got to the edge of town, before I finally saw the glow of my own windows in the distance. When I finally reached the house and exploded through the front door, everyone was crowded into the living room, singing carols.

Maybe it was that I reeked of wine, or maybe it was the look on my face, but I think right away everyone knew something horrible had happened because the singing stopped abruptly and Mrs. Johansen, who'd been sitting by the tree, jumped up and searched the space behind me with her eyes.

"Where's Katie?" she asked.

Just about the whole town raced with me through the woods. My eyes strained for the first sign of the lake, and then I saw the little lump that was Katie, still resting against the ice.

"Thank you, God, thank you, God," I chanted to myself, all the way up to the lake's edge. There I was abruptly brought to a halt by Mr. Johansen's outstretched arm. Giving me a ferocious look that told me to stay put, he padded out onto the ice alone.

"Katie!" he called. Behind us, a couple of the men had arrived with one of the barn ladders and now they began pushing it out toward Katie's daddy. He took hold of the bottom rung, slid the end out to where Katie's head and shoulders were still peeking out above the ice, and shimmied slowly toward her. Lunging over the last two rungs, he finally clasped Katie's hands, then her shoulders, and yelled back that he had her.

Three other men, including my daddy and Theo, grabbed on to the end of the ladder and pulled slowly, so slowly, as Mr. Johansen held on to Katie. It seemed to go on forever. Watching and waiting, I noticed that my teeth had stopped chattering. I felt like my whole body had gone completely still.

Doc Venable was waiting on the edge with his medical bag by the time they pulled Katie and her daddy in. Several people were sniffling and crying as he bent over her. Mr. Johansen stood behind him, wringing his hands. I had to peek through the cracks between people's bodies to see her, and when I did, my heart leapt into my throat. Her face was almost blue. She looked as tiny and delicate as a baby bird.

Doc Venable knelt there for a good few minutes, breathing into her mouth, then holding her limp wrist against his middle and forefinger. Finally he sat back on his heels.

Have you ever waited on someone who was about to say something really important to you? Waiting for them to breathe in and open their mouth and form the words is just like torture.

Doc's eyes rolled from left to right, settling briefly on my own, and then shifted to Mrs. Johansen, who was kneeling beside him and clutching her daughter's hand, cupping it against her lips. But he didn't take a breath. He didn't form the words.

He simply shook his head.

That's when Mrs. Johansen screamed. Just screamed and screamed. She kept yelling, "No, no, no, no," and lots of other people were now sobbing out loud.

As if some string from my neck were attached to that one word she kept saying, my head kept shaking back and forth in rhythm. No, no, no, no.

This couldn't be happening. Katie would get up in a minute or two and tell everyone she'd been joking, and I'd be mad at her at first, but then I'd be so happy that we'd both start laughing and I'd give her the biggest, tightest hug. It had to happen that way. God had to make it happen that way.

I looked at the people crying around me. *My* eyes were dry because I knew that they had to be wrong. Because if they weren't, that would mean I'd never get to see or talk to or hug or joke with Katie ever again.

And it would mean that I'd killed my best friend.

CHAPTER SIX

I slept for days, feverish, tossing.

Every once in a while Mama's face or Teresa's or sometimes Theo's would loom out at me. One minute I'd be alone and then suddenly one of them would be sitting there beside my bed, hunkered down by the lamp, reading the Bible or knitting.

Sometimes I wasn't in my bed at all but on a cloud, and instead of floating across the sky the cloud would be sinking, sinking, sinking below the earth, and I would feel my stomach flip with the sensation of falling.

Daddy's face, too, made its way into my visions. His dark eyes were filled with pain and sorrow as he brushed my sweat-soaked hair from my forehead, held my hand, kissed my cheek with a gentleness I would have never believed he had in him. But whenever I was fully awake, he was gone, and I wondered if he had really been there at all.

And then the time came when I was able to sit up and recognize the blue bedroom walls around me, and the gauzy white curtains, the wardrobe, the extra blankets Katie always used when she slept over.

I knew Katie was gone. Even in the sleep and sickness of the past—hours? days?—I had never forgotten that she was gone. But still, the sharp new awareness that came with my waking was burning a hole inside me.

"Well, look who's up," Mama said from the doorway, a covered tray in her hands. She moved to the edge of my bed, a concerned smile on her face, and arranged the tray on my lap, pulling off a dishcloth to reveal chicken stew and a cup of milk. I knew I couldn't eat a bite of it.

"What day is it, Mama?" I asked, my voice coming out in a croak. I cleared my throat.

"It's Wednesday, honey. It's New Year's Eve."

Seven days. I'd been asleep for seven days. Katie was buried by now.

"Mrs. Johansen?" I asked, hoping my mother understood what I meant because I couldn't say more.

"She's doing all right. Not good, of course, but she and the family are bearing up."

"I want to go see her," I said.

Mama tucked a stray hair behind her ear. Her face looked older than it ever had, and wrinkles stood out around her mouth. She sighed. "I don't think that's a good idea, Glory."

She stared at me for a second or two, then cleared her throat. "They've called a town meeting, honey. To discuss Katie's . . . to discuss what happened to Katie."

At the word *meeting,* the thing that jumped into my head wasn't a question or a protest. It was the memory of the sound of Lance King's mother crying when she found out her son was dead—a sound that was pure misery. I felt all the sick, hot-and-cold feelings of the previous days roil up again. I was pretty sure I was going to be sick, even though there was no food in my stomach to throw up. Mama was trying to remain calm, talking as if this were not as bad as it seemed, but now that I was more alert I could tell that underneath her calm smile, she was wildly afraid. She looked, the more I thought about it, like she hadn't slept in days.

There were only ever a few reasons for a town meeting. Since we all saw each other all the time, anyway, meetings were only held in the case of emergencies or on very serious matters. Like a trial.

In Dogwood's trials you didn't get put in jail or even sentenced to do extra chores. A trial meant one thing and one thing only—that you had done something horribly, terribly wrong. Either you'd be forgiven or given up. Sent away forever. Cast out. Like Lance King.

I didn't remember him, really. I just remembered that day with his mama crying, and feeling that something very terrible and very private had happened. All the kids made guesses on what he had done, but nobody knew for sure, and the grown-ups wouldn't say. But every once in a while if you were being bad, a grown-up would whisper, "Watch you don't end up like Lance King." Like Mrs. White had said to me, not six weeks before.

"Shhh," Mama said, seeing the rising fear on my face. "We're lucky you're alive, Glory. You almost died, you know. Your fever was so high."

After I didn't respond, she held me to her and kissed me on the forehead. But it couldn't stop the fear. And it couldn't stop the realization that being cast out, something I'd always considered a terrible, even unthinkable thing, was better than I deserved.

"'This, too, shall pass,'" Mama quoted. "As long as you're still with us, we can handle everything else."

I nodded agreement. But I knew this would never pass.

The town meeting was scheduled as soon I could walk and move around freely. The evening it was to happen, Mama, Theo, and I scrambled around the house getting ready as Teresa bundled little Marie up for the cold. I felt so ill that I hadn't eaten anything but a tiny breakfast I'd had to choke down.

"Don't forget your wool scarf, Glory," Mama said.

"What for? We're just going to the church," Theo argued.

"She needs to keep warm!" Mama said sharply. "Glory, get your scarf." She took my coat from my hands so I could go upstairs.

At the wardrobe, scarf in hand, I paused in front of the mirror.

My dark hair was braided into a tight pigtail that disappeared behind the collar of my best dress. My face was as white as a sheet, almost blue, and skinnier than I could ever remember it—making my chin look pointy. My eyes were big and empty, and they had dark bluish circles underneath. I didn't look like a young girl anymore. I looked more like a ghost.

I turned and rushed back downstairs.

We'd put off leaving until the last possible minute, and now we were going to be late. Daddy had gone a while ago to get things organized over at the church, which doubled as our town meeting hall. Before he'd left, he'd given me a quick kiss on the top of my head. But besides that, I hadn't seen much of him since coming out of my fever. He always seemed to be running around on some town matter or other, even more than usual. When I did see him, he didn't say much, and I couldn't tell whether the look he had was worry or disappointment, but I figured it was disappointment. We hadn't talked about Katie at all.

In fact, none of us had talked about Katie or about the meeting—other than discussing when it would be. It was like if all of us ignored these things, they wouldn't be true. We hadn't been talking much at all. But everyone had been extra sweet to me, with Teresa offering to do all my chores and Theo jumping up whenever I needed something—a pair of socks, a blanket, some more wool for the sweater I was knitting for Mrs. Johansen.

My mind was a blank. Sometimes I could almost forget that Katie was gone—as if being in this house, in the common room, knitting, were the only thing that had ever happened and would ever happen. But then I would flash back to being here with Katie the night before the Christmas party, and it was impossible to escape the knowledge that I'd lost her. Still, that was all I could understand, and the only things that reminded me time was still moving forward were the wilting and drying of the Christmas ornaments—the tree, the wreaths, the holly.

Finally we had ourselves collected, and my family and I walked out into the snow. It didn't occur to me to take a look back at my house, as if it were the last time I would see it. That didn't seem possible.

In fact, as we walked over to the church, the whole thing seemed like a dream. I felt like a character in a story that couldn't be real. The fear I'd felt when Mama first told me about the trial had given way to something else—this drifty distance in my head—from everyone and everything. It didn't matter what happened to me. Nothing mattered. It was like my heart and body were separated, like they were strangers to each other. Like I didn't know myself.

A few latecomers were straggling into the church ahead of us, but no one turned to look at us as we caught up. When we walked in through the big double doors, my mama took hold of my freezing-cold hands, which I'd forgotten to put into mittens, and the whole room fell into a sudden hush. I could feel my face going red, then pale, as everybody stared at me. Fear and nervousness beat a drum inside my stomach—far away, but there. I felt a warmth slip over my shoulders, and I realized Mama was covering my coat with her own. I thought vaguely how strange that was, since we were indoors now.

There was a bench in the front of the room that had clearly been left empty for me, and as I headed toward it, the rest of my family fell back. I hadn't known I would have to sit alone. The drumbeats inside me got faster as I turned to watch Mama, Theo, and Teresa, with Marie in her arms, take the nearest empty seats. Swallowing, I turned, walked toward the bench, and sat down.

Daddy, who I noticed now had been standing in the front of the room, cleared his throat and headed toward the Reverend's podium. Everyone quieted down even more.

"Glory Bee Mason," Daddy began, "you have been called here today in the eyes of the Lord and of your neighbors to be judged for the crime you have committed. This crime is the drinking of spirits, a grave sin in the eyes of God, and the resulting death"—at this word he swallowed, and I heard a cry from somewhere that must have been Mrs. Johansen—"the death of Katherine Ruth Johansen, one of the daughters of this town. Do you understand your crime?"

For the first time Daddy met my eyes, and I realized I was supposed to speak. The look he gave me made me feel like he was a stranger and not my own daddy. Like everything else, it didn't seem real. "Yes, sir," I whispered.

"Today the town of Dogwood will decide whether to forgive you, take you into its bosom and help you do penance for your evil ways, or to cast you out on the mercy of God. If you are cast out, you will be made to drink the Water of Judgment, according to the custom of our forefathers. Do you understand?"

I tried hard to make sense of these words, as my vision seemed to go black around the edges for a second or two. The Water of Judgment. The stories all said it was poison, and it meant certain death. But if that were true, how could Daddy look so calm up there saying I might have to drink it? Maybe he felt as far away as I did.

Something made my head nod, and I felt like a puppet.

"We will open this matter to a discussion. At the end of the discussion, we will have a vote to decide on your fate. Who would like to talk first?" Daddy's eyes searched the congregation.

I blinked as Theo shot to his feet. "Glory never meant for harm to come to Katie," he said, the words rushing out of him like meltwater in the spring. "It was an accident. She's real, real sorry."

Abruptly he sat down. His cheeks were patched with red, and

he was breathing like he'd just run a mile. I tried to smile at him, but somehow I couldn't get the corners of my mouth to go up.

There was a rustle, and everyone shifted their attention to Reverend Clifton, who stood up, his hands clasped in front of him. "As the spiritual leader of this community," he said in the same booming voice he used for church, "I have seen the devil in Glory Mason from a very young age and made warnings about what it would lead to. I am sure Miss Mason regrets what she's done, and why wouldn't she?"

I was no longer looking at the Reverend—I was studying my own feet, noticing all the scuffs and scratches on the toes of my boots. The Reverend's voice rose.

"Glory Mason has murdered—yes, *murdered*—one of our own. She must pay the price for what she's done. An eye for an eye." With that, several voices rose up—some in agreement, some in anger.

You can't imagine what it's like to see people you've grown up with, even your very own family, arguing on whether or not you should be sent away to die. It's like one of those nightmares you are so glad to wake up from, to see that everything is still right with the world after all. This was like that, only I couldn't seem to wake. There was no rightness in it at all. But there was no wrongness, either. Just emptiness and driftiness and, buried way down deep, panic.

"Excuse me," said a woman's voice in the back of the room.

I twisted to see Mrs. White standing up and felt my stomach drop with the certainty of the bad things she would say. *Not happening. Not really happening,* I told myself. Maybe my fever had come back. Maybe it was all a fever dream. The crowd rustled behind me.

Mrs. White's cheeks were white and papery looking, just like her hair. Her mouth was tight in a scowl. "I for one have always thought Miss Glory Mason to be ornery as homemade sin," she began, "and I knew something like this was bound to happen. I told her so, and I told her parents so, too, and this tragedy is no fault of mine." She paused for a moment as a few people whispered to each other. Then she said, "But Glory is just a child, and it's clear that regret for what she's done will be with her for her whole life, and with all due respect to the Johansens, sending Glory away will not bring Katie back."

There was a brief rustle as everyone absorbed what had been said. I just stared. I was surprised, but not relieved—because a feeling like that would have been real, and nothing was real.

My gaze drifted to the Johansens. Mrs. Johansen looked awful—all pale with red, raw eyes. I tried to catch her gaze, but she was staring fixedly at a spot high over my head. The children looked lost and forlorn. Only Thomas, googly-eyed Thomas, sent a glare back my way, making me lower my eyes in shame.

But it was Mr. Johansen's face that had struck me most. His eyes weren't red and puffy; his face wasn't anything less than its usual ruddy, strong color; he didn't look lost. He looked enraged.

When he stood up, the room fell dead quiet.

"I'm no spiritual leader," he said firmly. "I'm no great judge of character. If I was, I would have"—his eyes welled up with tears—"I would have steered my Katie away from Glory Mason. But I didn't. And all I know is, my daughter was only thirteen years old, and now she's gone."

Several folks in the audience let out choking sighs and sniffles. "And the girl who's responsible for it is sitting up there, and you're thinking of letting her stay because she's *sorry*," he went on. His voice caught. "Well, I'm sorry, too, for ever knowing her. We cast people out when they do things we can't forgive them for. What is more unforgivable than this?"

Mrs. Johansen reached up and clutched her husband's hand. I couldn't tell whether she was trying to calm him or to back up what he was saying.

"Glory Mason is bad for this town," Mr. Johansen said. "She will always be bad for this town. I don't care how sorry she is. She can't change what's in her heart, and that's carelessness and selfishness. For that reason, she needs to go."

No voices rose up to protest Mr. Johansen's words. And the thing was, I knew he was right. The Glory who cared whether I lived or died had curled up in a ball inside me, and there was only this part of me that knew he was right. No one spoke for several minutes, even though my daddy searched the crowd for anyone wanting to argue.

Finally he rested his hands on the sides of the podium. "If no one has anything more to say, we will put this matter to a vote." He looked around the room. "All who wish Glory Mason to stay a part of our community, and practice penance as the town sees fit, say aye."

"Aye," a few voices rang out. Among them I recognized my mother's voice, cracking.

"All those in favor of casting Glory Mason out, according to our customs, upon the mercy of God, say aye."

"Aye." The sound was overwhelming. The voices were so many that I could not separate one voice from the chorus.

There was a long, long silence, not only in the crowd, but also inside of me—like my soul had drained out and away. Daddy stood like a statue, staring at some unknown point behind me. I'd never seen him like this before, and I knew he had removed himself completely from this moment. Because how could the man about to do this to me also be my daddy? Then he spoke, and his voice was dry, dead, like twigs breaking.

"Glory Bee Mason, you have been cast out of the town of Dogwood and sentenced to drink the Water of Judgment, according to custom. Stand up." Suddenly there was a noise behind me, and I turned to see several folks catching my mama, who had fainted dead away.

I don't know how I stood up, because I couldn't feel my legs.

"Come forward," Daddy said in that awful, toneless voice.

The Reverend had risen, too, and approached the brass vial, which I now noticed was sitting on the altar. I could hear several people sobbing, but it seemed like they were all a million miles away. I kept my eyes on my daddy, who looked suddenly so old—a lot like my grandpa had before he died.

The Reverend walked toward me, pulling out the cork to the vial. He came to a stop directly in front of me. "Glory Mason, I will explain to you the course of the punishment that has been given you." He indicated the vial, holding it in both hands.

"At first," he said, "you will feel no change. Then you will want to sleep. Later you'll develop the symptoms of a cold—coughing, weakness, fever. This is the beginning of your body's breakdown, which will continue for months, perhaps as long as a year, until the poison has its ultimate effect: death."

Death. The word seemed to echo inside my head.

"You must not attempt to find a cure through medicine or modern doctors, because this will not help you, and it is against God's will. Your fate, once you drink the water, is sealed." With a somber look, the Reverend raised the vial in front of his face and started chanting, saying something in a language I couldn't understand. I guess it must have been Latin.

As one of our many projects long ago, Katie and I had made a planter for the front of the church. It rested right under the tall church window at the back of the altar, and it contained a forget-me-not—Katie's favorite. A few months after we'd planted it, it had mysteriously died. Well, not that mysteriously. I had been in charge of watering it, and I'd forgotten. Katie had dragged it out behind her house, planning to use the pot it was in for something else, but she never got around to it.

Then one day, about a year later, we'd been out back and noticed some bits of green sticking out of the dried-up dirt. Katie ran to get a watering pitcher, and soon enough, that flower had come back bigger and more beautiful than before. Now it was resting right back where it had started, at the front of the church, and seeing it there somehow sparked something inside my emptiness. The plant was alive. And Katie was dead. Dead, dead, dead, dead, dead.

Suddenly I broke out of the daze I'd been in for the past hour—for the past many days—and brought my hand to my mouth to hold back a cry. The ache inside me was unbearable. Katie was dead and I was being poisoned, being sent away forever.

Everything in me screamed, "No!" as the Reverend held the vial to my lips, but I tilted my head back all the same and felt the liquid running down my throat. I thought it would burn, but it tasted like nothing at all. Like death.

Oh, God.

"This meeting is over," my father said, his voice still dry and toneless. He walked to the big front doors of the church and flung them open. "Let us go home and think on the loss of our daughter, Glory." Then he walked out into the night, alone.

I half expected to fall down dead right there on the spot, but it didn't happen. I desperately looked around the room. I wanted to bury my head against my mama. I needed to. I needed *someone,* just to hold me. But I noticed that no one was looking back at me. People were getting up, getting out of their seats, and actually making their way to the door. *The loss of our daughter.* Many folks were sobbing like they were at a funeral. Like I was dead.

I *was* dead.

I stood for another moment or two, trying to make sense of it all in my head. Trying to figure out a way it could possibly make sense. I noticed that beyond the windows, snowflakes had once again begun to fall. The back door of the church hung open. Obviously it had been left that way for me—so my leaving could be as invisible as possible.

"Please," I whispered.

Nobody looked at me. Everyone was shuffling out the front doors and away, leaving me.

"Mama?" I called, running to tug on my mother's sweater, but she just let her head fall into her hands as Theo dragged her away. He and Teresa wouldn't look at me either. Only little Marie turned her head as she was carried through the door. Seeing me, she squealed, and I grasped at her hand. "Marie," I whispered, and then they were gone.

The church was suddenly completely quiet. As far as I could tell, not a soul was left inside. Already I felt I was here only as a ghost, that I was only haunting this place. I watched my family, five miniature people floating away downhill. We had been six, just an hour before. I hadn't even gotten to tell them good-bye, and now it seemed more important than anything. But it was too late.

I closed the main doors behind them carefully, making sure to hitch the knob just right, like I used to do when I was helping the Reverend with Sunday school.

Then I ran out the back, into the snow.

CHAPTER
SEVEN

I ran and ran and ran. I didn't feel the cold biting into my face. I didn't see the snow rushing at me.

I would have run forever if I could have, because it seemed somehow like I might be able to outrun my feelings. But finally I had to slow to a walk, huffing and panting, my breath turning into frozen crystals in the night.

I stumbled along through the woods, getting farther and farther away from home, the snow sloshing into the tops of my boots. My coat, overlapped by Mama's heavier one, was unbuttoned and hung open to the cold. My scarf trailed behind me, attached to me only by a thread. I didn't think to pull it around me.

Sure enough, as I slowed down, my thoughts caught up with me. Tears started to stream down my cheeks finally, uncontrollably. I let out the cry I'd been holding in at the town meeting, a long, slow groan, followed by another and another. I didn't bother to swipe at the tears, though the liquid felt bitingly cold as it coursed down my cheeks, making my face that much more sensitive to the wind.

I won't try to tell you all that I was feeling then. It's impossible to explain what it feels like to lose your best friend and your family and your home, and to know that it was all your fault. I *will* tell you what I was thinking, though. I was thinking that I should have never been born.

I went on like that for a long, long time, aching, hating myself more than I'd ever hated anyone. My tears finally ran out, even though I didn't feel any better. Finally I started looking around, wondering where I was.

I'd run deep into the woods—in which direction, I wasn't sure. Where was I going? What was I going to do? I didn't want to *do* anything. I just wanted to disappear. The only thing that I could think of was to go find the frozen lake where Katie had died and throw myself in so I could go to sleep forever with her. But then I remembered that Katie was surely in heaven and there was no place in heaven for someone like me.

I also realized I didn't know which way the lake was. I'd always known these woods like the back of my hand, but now they seemed strange to me. I could be miles from the lake by now—I had no earthly idea.

I stopped and stood, looking about me for a sign of something, anything familiar. I spun in all different directions, and all I could see was snow, trees, and more trees. My tears burst out again, and I sank right there in that spot, onto my knees, my bare hands sunk in the snow. That's when I gave up.

There was no point. There was nowhere I wanted to go.

The poison didn't even seem to matter now because it wouldn't have time to do its job. Nature would do it instead, and I wouldn't try to stop it. I prayed that it would be quick. I prayed to God to help me handle the little bit of time I had left.

"God, please help me. God, please help me," I said over and over again. How long I'd been kneeling here, repeating it, I did not know. It could have been hours. Or seconds. But suddenly everything around me seemed to go still. I didn't hear the wind anymore. I didn't hear the trees creaking in the January air.

Am I dying? I thought. *Is this what it's like?*

And then came another thought: *God helps those who help themselves.*

It wasn't that I'd never heard that phrase before. I'd heard it a million times, and it had never had much meaning for me. But this time it shook me. I mean, shook me inside. And then there came a tiny inkling of strength—something I definitely did not have in me until that second. It wasn't much, it wasn't nearly anything like happiness or even like wanting to live, but it was enough to make me stand up and keep walking.

At first I thought it was a mirage. It was nestled within a large clump of mountain laurel, which keeps its greenery all year round, so thick that the snow hardly penetrated it. Above the grouping of bushes, a long tree limb hung horizontal to the ground. And against and around this limb were the remains of a shelter.

It was shaped like a long triangle. Its slanted roof-walls were made out of long strips of bark, boughs of dried-up pine, dirt, and dry leaves, leaning up against the horizontal limb like a kind of teepee. The snow only lightly dusted it, since most anything that fell on it was rolling down its tilted surface onto the ground.

I burrowed through the thick undergrowth, feeling suddenly that whether I lived or died depended on getting into that shelter as soon as possible. It didn't occur to me that a few minutes ago, living hadn't seemed important to me. What would I find inside? What were the chances that the snow wasn't just leaking through the shabby roof and that it would be just as cold as anywhere else in this forest?

As I rested my numb fingers gently on the roof of the lean-to, I sent another silent prayer to God, asking him to make this work. Then I ducked and looked for the entrance. It was hard to find, as brambles grew thickly around it, but soon enough, there it was—a small triangle, just big enough for my body to fit through if I crouched.

Within the clump of bushes, the howling of the wind had lessened to a dull moan, and now that I put my head inside the shelter, it died almost completely. It was dark inside and, forgetting to worry about snakes or other creatures that might be burrowing there, I ran my hands along the ground. I breathed a sigh of relief. Though bits of snow had piled up here and there, the ground was mostly dry.

Slowly I crawled inside. The air felt warm compared to the harsh weather outside, though I'm sure it couldn't have been above freezing. I curled up against the far wall, finally finding enough sense to button up my mama's coat. The coat was big enough for me to pull my head down inside it, and as I did so, I yanked my hands in through the sleeves. The more I breathed, the warmer it became inside my little cocoon. I pulled my knees up to my chest, tucking my hands between them and trying to keep in as much heat as possible.

Now that I had stopped moving, the exhaustion of the day hit me. I was more tired than I'd ever been. I was colder than I'd ever been. I was, of course, more miserable than I'd ever been. I had only a second to think about it as my body slowly shut down and darkness closed around my brain, but I guessed it was a day for breaking records.

And then I fell into a black, cold sleep.

When I woke, I thought I heard Mama downstairs making breakfast. I was impressed with myself for waking up early for once. I was going to go downstairs and pitch in with the cooking. I'd been bad recently, a do-less like the Reverend said, but today I was going to start trying to be better.

Only something was wrong. It was too cold in the house. My

legs felt all stiff when I stretched them. Slowly I opened my eyes and realized that of course I wasn't in my house at all. Above me, slanting sunlight leaked through bits of bark and moss. Bitter cold nipped at my feet and legs and any other part of my body that wasn't hidden inside my thick wool coat. And then it hit me.

Katie.

I pulled my head back into my collar and tried to go back to that place I'd just been, that lovely dream of grits and eggs and coffee and my mama downstairs and everybody still loving me like they used to. But it was no use. My heart hurt like someone was scraping it with a poker.

I sat up and looked around me, longing for something to take my mind off my sadness. The shelter I was in was larger than I'd thought last night. Whoever had made it had obviously stayed in it for a while 'cause there was a dent in the ground where a little bed had been hollowed out. There were even a few utensils, half buried next to the wall—a tin mug, a hunting knife. I wondered if this had been a hideout for hunters, waiting to sight their prey, but it seemed too low to the ground for that. I even thought about it being left over from Indian times, but then I realized it would have rotted away long ago.

My thoughts were interrupted by the growl of my belly, which hadn't had anything in it since yesterday morning. I ignored it. There wasn't any use, I figured, in feeding a dying belly. It would only make it take longer to starve, which I wanted to happen as quickly and painlessly as possible.

I picked up the knife and fiddled with it. Then I grabbed the tin mug and picked at the murky, dirty bottom of it with my own dirty fingernails. I tugged at the snarls in my hair, which were caked together with dirt and sap and whatever else I had brushed against in my frenzy the night before.

Then I realized there was no point in cleaning up, and that made me burst into tears. My throat hurt from crying so much the night before, but that didn't slow me down—even though it didn't seem possible that I could have any liquid left in me.

Finally the tears went away. I lay back down on the floor and tried, once again, to go to sleep. Waiting out my death was going to be horrible, and I wanted to spend most of it unconscious. Still, sleep wouldn't come. I still felt hungry. I had to *go*.

Reluctantly I got up and went outside to the bushes. The snow had stopped, and all around me were woods upon woods that still looked as unfamiliar to me as they had last night. The sun was shining cold and bitter, or at least that's the way it seemed. Birds were even chirping.

Suddenly I was madder than hell. How could everything be so normal out here when everything was different for me? Was the world moving on without Katie? Was that how it was?

I looked up at the blue sky as if I were looking straight at God. I forgot about praying to Him the night before and asking Him to help me. I just made fists of my hands and glared.

Then I ducked back into my shelter.

I waited and waited for the day to pass. How long did it take for a person to starve? How could I make it go faster? Was there a way to speed up the poison? I racked my brains for a memory of the Reverend or the other town elders mentioning it in all their long lectures. Nothing came to mind. Well, I deserved to die slow, I guessed.

As I thought, my cold fingers wandered into my mama's coat pockets and happened upon something I hadn't expected.

The pockets were stuffed.

My pulse speeding up, I yanked out the strange bulges in both pockets and laid them in front of me one by one. There were mittens. A hat. Inside the hat was an apple and a chunk of cheese. Inside each mitten were two biscuits.

When I thought I'd got everything, I fished one more time into the seams just in case, and my hands came across a cardboard square that made my heart lurch even before I saw it. I knew now that my mama must have packed all this stuff, knowing what was likely to happen at the town meeting, and I knew what I now held in my hand. I slowly pulled it out and, taking in a breath, turned it over.

There, in their best clothes, were the members of the Mason family, smiling brightly at the camera. It had been taken with an old black-and-white camera before little Marie was born. There was Teresa dressed neatly as usual in a dress she had made herself. There was Theo in coveralls, shorter and more baby-faced than now but wearing his usual smirk. There was Mama, her hair pulled back and the look on her face tired but happy. There I was, around nine or ten years old, staring off to the side of the camera at something, I didn't remember what, that was making me laugh. And there was Daddy, standing head and shoulders above us, looking proud and protective of his little family.

I touched each of the faces and tucked the picture back inside my pocket. Then I set to ignoring the food in front of me. My belly, knowing it was dinnertime, was setting up a bigger protest than it had all day. My brain still wanted me to starve.

My brain held out until it was almost dark, but finally my belly won. I grabbed the hunk of cheese and swallowed it in about three bites, then started on the apple. I ate everything but one of the biscuits.

So much for willpower. I put it on my list of things to hate about myself.

Dusk turned into night, and pretty soon I was lying back in the dirt, my feet scrunched up to my belly. I'd put on my hat and mittens and wrapped my scarf around my face, but it was much harder to get to sleep than it had been the night before, even though I was still exhausted.

My mind kept coming back to Katie, as if she weren't there at the back of it every second, anyway. With my eyes closed, I brought up her face in my mind. I kept thinking of Christmas Eve, piecing it all together like a story over and over again, to see if I could make the end come out different. But it never changed. It was still my fault, all my fault. Not that there had been any doubt of that, but the more I thought on it, my actions seemed careless and reckless and evil.

I reached down into my coat pocket and pulled the photo of my family up to my cheek in the dark. Maybe, by holding it close to me, I could somehow send my spirit to Dogwood, to wrap my spirit arms around my family.

With that thought, I found some kind of comfort, and the hot-poker feeling in my chest eased enough to let me sleep.

CHAPTER
EIGHT

Somewhere in the late morning of the next day, I set about fixing up my shelter. I figured it wouldn't hurt to make it a bit warmer and more livable while I waited to die. I peeled bark off the surrounding trees with the help of my new knife, dug up mud and moss up to pack into the crevices, then covered that with a thick layer of snow, which I knew from Daddy could actually make a shelter warmer, even though the snow itself was so cold. I gathered bunches of pine boughs to cover the dirt floor and put an extra-large stack of them in the hollow where I would sleep. I even fashioned a cover for the entrance out of strips of bark that I wove together like a basket.

Once that was done, I cleaned my tin mug and filled it with snow and set it near me in the shelter so my body heat would help to melt it. Then I went back to sitting and waiting. But sitting still made the feeling in my heart so much worse that I set about doing more chores. I gathered rocks to make a fire pit beside my shelter, not really knowing how I'd make the fire to go in it. At home there was always a fire going, so anything you needed to light, you lit from that. I hoped I'd be able to do it on my own, just by remembering how Daddy did it when he used to take me on hunting trips, before he decided I should start staying home with the women.

What with all the snow, it was hard to find wood that was even close to being dry. Still, I gathered what I could of little sticks and kindling and made a pile indoors. On these forages I picked berries and nuts I recognized—bearberries, a few rare beechnuts that hadn't already fallen or been taken by squirrels. I nibbled on them, reasoning that it wouldn't be enough to keep me alive but would at least keep my hunger pangs at bay.

It didn't work, though. The hunger was there when I woke up the next morning and the morning after that. It went on for three days, so long that hunger was on my mind even more than Katie now and more than my determination to starve to death. I'd eaten the last biscuit at some point during the night because I was feeling so dizzy and queasy, and now there was nothing. I couldn't keep on like this. I needed and wanted to eat. And to do that, I needed to get a fire going.

Even though I hadn't really admitted it to myself, my foraging missions had also become missions to find the way home. I couldn't go back there to live, but maybe I could just sneak in to grab a few of the items I needed—some dry kindling from the storehouse, some cheese maybe, some dried meat. Would that be stealing? It didn't seem like it, but now that I was an outsider, maybe it was.

It didn't matter anyhow. My searches had turned up nothing familiar, and now I was getting too weak to even try.

Finally, on the third day, I took a bunch of kindling from the pile I'd made and carried it to the fire pit. Maybe it was dry enough to burn by now. I arranged the wood carefully in the way I remembered Daddy doing it, like a teepee, with the bigger wood on top and kindling underneath and a small pile of wood shavings on top of that for tinder. Then I sat on the ground with a wide piece of wood on my lap and started digging a long groove out of it with my knife. Daddy had always made it look so easy, but even just that one little step took forever.

Once that was done, I tilted the wood so that the end of the groove rested on the unlit fire. I took a thin, strong stick I'd chosen and began rubbing it along the groove. For a long time I rubbed and rubbed that stick against the wood as fast as I could. And nothing. After a few minutes' rest I tried again, for as long as my arms would let me.

Nothing. The end of the wood and the tip of the stick were smoking a little, but the pile in front of me stayed the same. Nothing at all was happening. My arm muscles ached, and my hands stung.

That evening, after a long, cold nap, I was at it again. The constant scraping was slowly working its way into my head, making me feel like my mind was scraping around inside my skull. I felt like I was going to lose my balance and fall over, and I decided I should probably give up before that happened. The wood was probably too wet. The tinder . . .

"Uhhh," I gasped, slapping my forehead.

I took my knife and sliced into a dry part of my skirt, just above the hem, tearing off a section about the size of my hand. Then I arranged it in the middle of my fire, underneath the teepee of logs I had built. This was what Daddy did during the rainy season, when finding dry tinder was impossible. I'd clean forgotten.

Once again I started rubbing. Before long, the stick's tip started to give out a wispy stream of smoke, and hot little bits of wood dust flew onto the cloth. My heartbeat quickened, seeming to keep up the rhythm of my movements as I rubbed the stick faster and faster.

Finally a bit of the cloth began to smoke and blacken, curling up at the edges. I leaned down and blew a tiny breath, ever so slightly, at the now smoking bit of material. Those seconds seemed to go by so slowly, but sure enough, the cloth began burning in earnest, and a tiny point in the nest of twigs above it started to glow orange. Soon a tiny flame, and then two, licked along one of the sticks.

Fire! I'd had no idea something so simple could ever make me so happy. After making sure the flame was caught, I ran to get some more wood. Triumphantly I wiped my sweaty face and noticed the blood on my hands. I had scraped them raw.

For some reason, it made me proud. For a minute I even forgot to be sad.

On my fourth day, I caught a fish.

It wasn't much of a fish, but it hadn't been much of a pond I'd gotten it from. I'd found the pond that morning. It was covered in a layer of ice, but ice fishing wasn't new to me. Theo and I had done it at the lake lots of times, and it didn't take long for me to melt a hole through the ice and cast a line made out of thread from the hem of my dress and a hook I'd fashioned with a rusty nail I found near the water. Luckily I was good at finding worms for bait.

Back at my camp, I cleaned and gutted the croaker, stuck it onto a couple of beech sticks I'd sharpened, and grilled it just long enough so I knew it wouldn't make me throw up. Then I tore into it like it was the first meal I'd ever had. I can't say it was the most delicious because I didn't even taste it going down. I felt guilty eating, and being so excited about it, too, when I had been set on letting myself starve. But I couldn't think about that too much. My body wanted to live, no matter what the rest of me was telling it.

I went on like this for a few days, eating nuts and berries during the day and settling down to a fish dinner at dusk. Every night when I went to sleep, I thought about Katie and said a million *sorry*s, chanting the word until I drifted off. I didn't cry anymore. It was like the ache was too deep inside for tears.

I certainly didn't pray. I'd resolved, in all these hours and hours of thinking, not to be friends with God ever again. Even if I had Him to thank for guiding me to this shelter and helping me to find food, I would never forgive Him for taking Katie, even though her going was mostly my fault. He could have let her live if He'd wanted to. And so, even if I paid for my anger with eternal damnation after a death that wasn't so very far away, I was not going to give God one more ounce of my friendship, ever.

I thought about the Johansens a lot. I knew they all must hate me. But it hurt me the most to think of Mrs. Johansen feeling like that, because I loved her almost the way I loved my own mama. Maybe hating me would make her feel a little better about Katie somehow. I didn't know how that would work, but I hoped it would.

I thought a lot about myself. Ever since I could remember, folks in town had been telling me that I was a rotten apple and that my mischief would amount to something terrible someday. And it had. I'd thought I was right standing up for myself, but all the time it turned out the Reverend and the rest of them were right instead.

Why couldn't I have listened?

I'd started to notch my days onto the limb that made up the center of the shelter's roof—to help me remember how long I'd been here but also to mark off the number of days of my life, the days to be subtracted from the time I had left. I was very careful about it, and that's how I know that my seventh day was when I found the initials.

I was crawling inside with a stack of wood, and I banged my knee on a bit of rock that was sticking out of the soil just inside the entrance. I curled into a ball, grabbing at my knee. My foot knocked a big piece of bark out of place. And that's when I saw the letters *L. B. K.* notched into the wood of the center pole, clear as day.

L. B. K. I forgot about my knee, sat up, and traced the letters with my fingers. Who was he? What had this place been to him? What had happened to him?

Whoever he was, a hunter or someone, he had saved my life in a way, at least temporarily. I hoped he was happy, wherever he was.

The rest of the day I didn't feel quite so alone. A lot of my time I now spent sitting by the fire. That evening I sat and thought of L. B. K. I felt like he was there, too, sitting with me in the silence of the woods.

It wasn't until that night, tucked inside my coat, that I realized who L. B. K. was.

I jerked upright, clutching the space over my heart. And then I started sobbing, hard, hiccupping sobs. L. B. K. wasn't a hunter. He wasn't somewhere happy like I'd hoped. He was

Lance King. Of course. He'd been sent away from the village of Dogwood and poisoned, just like me. And he was dead!

It was all such a waste—Katie and Lance King and me. We were youngsters with our whole lives ahead of us . . . until suddenly it was all at an end. The unfairness of it all closed around me, making me feel like I couldn't breathe.

I stared at the walls of the shelter Lance King had made so carefully, at the tin mug he'd drunk from, at the space he'd hollowed out for a bed. And it struck me with sudden sureness that Lance King had wanted to live. Even when everything he cared about was gone.

"I don't want to die." I said it out loud, and the sound of my own voice startled me. I hadn't heard it in so long. I realized that over the past week, under all the thoughts about Katie and home and wasting away to sleep forever, I'd been afraid.

"I don't want to die!" I said it again, a little lower. "Glory Mason, Glory Mason, Glory Mason," I chanted. I didn't really know why. I guess it was like hearing my own name made me feel like I had someone with me, a friend.

Myself.

I stayed up late into the night, sitting by the fire, looking at the stars. I stayed up until the moon was getting lower to the horizon, until even the owls weren't whooing anymore. But I wasn't just thinking about how sad I was, how sad everything was. I wasn't thinking about things that I could never change. I was thinking on a problem and figuring out a solution.

My brain was working on a plan. And early next morning that plan would be as clear as day, though now under the stars, in the smoke of the fire, it only seemed like a hope, a dream, a wish. But really, it was a plan.

A plan on how, exactly, I was going to get to Boston.

CHAPTER
NINE

You wouldn't think it to look at him, but my daddy is an educated man. I don't know where he learned all the stuff he did, since there were hardly any books in Dogwood, but he knows all about the ancient Greeks and their beliefs about the stars. When I was a little girl and we were out on one of Daddy's deer-hunting trips, I used to lie by the fire with my head on his belly and he would stroke my hair and tell me all the different constellations: Orion, Cassiopeia, Taurus. I would pull his hand into mine and ask him question after question, hoping that those ancient Greeks were right and that there really were living gods and wild animals up there. That's how I'd learned that long-ago folks navigated by the stars, and why I could do it a little bit myself.

Late on the night I found Lance King's initials, I picked my path. I knew Boston was north, and with a little bit of thinking and remembering things Mrs. Johansen had told me, I also remembered it was to the east. So I'd used the stars to figure out which way northeast was. I'd packed my few things early the next morning, using my scarf as a sack to hold my tin mug and a croaker I'd smoked the night before. I slid my knife into my mama's coat pocket.

Now, walking northeast, I felt like I had a purpose for the first time since Katie died. It was like having a reason to keep moving and living and breathing for the time before the poison got me. I was going to make it to Boston, the place Katie and I had dreamed of going to, the place I'd *promised* to go to with her. I was going to fulfill my promise, even though things hadn't turned out exactly how we'd planned. I was going to Boston, and I was going to take Katie with me.

It wasn't that I thought I could make things up to her. Or that seeing Boston would ever mean one smidgen as much as having her back. It was just that making it there was the one thing I could give her. Maybe if one of us went, it would make her death mean something instead of being a pure waste, like Lance King's. Like mine.

Maybe that doesn't make much sense. And truly, I didn't know what it would all mean to Katie, if she was bothering to look down on me from heaven. But I would get there if it was the last thing I did. I'd see the buildings and the people and the cars and the contraptions. Like I'd promised.

I just hoped I had enough life left to make it there.

The woods were alive with cardinals, blue jays, squirrels—all the creatures that weren't sleeping the long winter away in comfy hidey-holes. Every once in a while I spotted a deer, delicate and skittish. My path meandered around fallen trees and big rocks, over small streams flowing with bits of melting snow, but always in one direction. The time dragged slowly as I walked. How many miles away was Boston? How many miles could I travel in one day?

It didn't occur to me until lunchtime that there were surely a bunch of towns between here and Boston. The nearest one I knew of, the one that some of the older folks used to talk about, was about seventy miles away by dirty mountain roads, although I didn't know in what direction it was or how far seventy miles really was. But surely, eventually, I'd run into a town. And then . . . what would I do? What were people from other towns like, anyway?

I'd always figured the Reverend was just exaggerating when he talked about how evil all the outsiders were, with their lying and robbing and cheating innocent Christians. But now I wondered if I shouldn't have taken it all a bit more seriously. I wished I'd asked more questions on how to figure out which strangers were good and which weren't.

I quieted my fears by telling myself that if I made it to a town, I'd be happy just to be among other living beings, good *or* bad.

Afternoon became evening. The walking was turning out to be a lot harder than I'd expected. My legs were hurting from the strain, and I felt drained of energy. I ached with longing for the little shelter I'd left. When I finally hunkered down for the night under the shelter of a towering pine tree, I was hungry again. I hadn't seen another pond like the one I'd gotten my fish from. There were only fast-running streams where not even arrowroot, which I could have boiled for food, would grow. I'd eaten a handful of chestnuts I'd collected from a few different trees, but there hadn't been many. Worry sent me to sleep. Where would I find real food? And what would happen to me with the coming harshness of winter?

When the sun got up, so did I. I'd been awake for a while, shivering in the cold, waiting for the first slim rays of dawn before rising and blowing warm air into my mittens and setting my fire. Now I sipped at a mug of hot water with pine needles mixed in for flavor, trying to forget the growling in my belly. Surely I would find a place to fish this day.

I started walking again. Time dragged on. The squirrels that zipped across nearby tree limbs every now and then with their acorns filled me with envy. And then there was another thought. What if I could catch one of them? I'd never killed an animal in my life, aside from fish, and the thought made me queasy. I liked meat well enough, but I didn't like to think of it having a cute little face.

Once again I resolved to think of other things to get my mind off how unhappy my body was. Putting one foot in front of the other had overtaken any sadder, more serious thoughts a while ago, and now, to keep my feet moving, I retreated into imagining better times. I tried my best to picture myself sitting by the woodstove in Mama's kitchen, my feet up on the grate (even though Daddy was always telling me I was going to set myself on fire doing that).

But the more I tried to imagine this, the more I ached for home, and the more I felt the distance growing between me and Dogwood like a stretching bit of elastic. I could keep getting farther and farther away, but one side of that elastic was tied to my heart, and the other was tied to home, and it felt like soon it would snap back—taking my heart with it and leaving me empty inside. I knew that even if I went home and begged for forgiveness, I wouldn't receive it. And every step I took seemed to make it that much more impossible ever to return.

I crested a big hill and surveyed the land for any sign of a change—a lake, or a house, or another living human being. Laid out before me were just trees and trees and more trees. It went on like this for a lot of the day. Though I took detours up streams to look for their sources, I found only rocky springs and no still water for fish to live in. I was getting weaker.

Another night of going to bed with an aching belly came and went.

It wasn't until the third day of walking, when there was still no sign of anyplace to get food, that the fear really began to settle in again. A question flitted around the back of my brain, and I willed it to stay back there so I wouldn't have to face it. It wanted to ask, What if I couldn't make it to Boston? What if I couldn't even make it to the next town? I couldn't think about how to answer a question like that.

But in spite of my best efforts to ignore the worry growing inside, somewhere along the way my goals began to change. Boston became smaller and smaller in my mind. I began to focus my hope on simply getting out of these mountains. It was starting to seem like that might not happen. I started resting every hour or so, too tired to find a dry place—just plumping right down on the snow. I looked at my arms, and they seemed so much scrawnier and weaker to me than they ever had, like little sticks. Whenever I stood up from one of these rests, my bones ached. The skin around my mouth and eyes felt tight and dry, my cheeks felt raw. My legs felt like they were floating below me, like I had no control over how fast they moved. Was I going to be walking forever, until I collapsed? Were they going to find my body in the woods, too?

No. No, no, no. I was going to Boston. I knew there had to be a town out there, if I could only keep moving.

Suddenly my stomach lurched and I knelt, heaving. Nothing came out. Did people heave like this when they starved? I got up once the spasms had passed, shuffling along now with one hand over my stomach and the other swinging at my side.

Slowly, slowly. The forest sounds seemed louder, I guess because I was making hardly any noise at all.

Then I heard it. Crackling. And a kind of low, moaning sound.

There was something to the left of me—a color that was out of place in all the white. It was an animal, but what kind?

My sight and hearing suddenly sharpened, trained on whatever it was behind the trees. I walked as softly as I could to a spot where I could see more clearly.

It was a red fox. I slumped in my spot. A fox wasn't a food option—not a practical one, anyway, because how would I catch it? But I stood there a minute longer, considering. And as I did, I realized the fox had something in his mouth.

I moved a little closer—so close, I could hear the fox's snuffling breath hissing in and out. He didn't even glance in my direction; he was too busy tearing into the poor, dead rabbit he'd caught. The poor, dead rabbit I wanted for myself. Lord, did I want it!

My breath sped up. The fox was so skinny, his ribs were sticking out. He looked about as starved as I felt. He was just trying to survive, but then, so was I.

Slowly I crouched, pulling off my mittens and digging around the ground with my hands. One small rock. Two. My aim was good, I knew. But what to do once I hit my mark? Wait for the fox to run away. He had to, because I was counting on it.

The longer I stood wondering, the more precious food would be gone, so without another thought I stepped into a better position, cocked back my arm, and hurled the first rock as hard as I could.

The yelp was so startling, I jumped. It was the loudest sound I'd heard since I'd come into the woods, and it took me a second to recover my wits. When I did, I saw the fox hadn't moved from his spot. He was standing, shaking, legs splayed over his prey, looking around for his attacker. I cocked back my arm to fling the second rock. The moment I did, he saw me.

Most animals, when they're faced with a human, will run away. Save their own skins. But foxes are among the nastier wild animals, the kind that don't need much to be provoked. And this one was desperate, on top of being provoked. I guess that's why he started running—not away, but straight in my direction. His teeth were bared.

"Ahhh!" Shocked, forgetting about my second rock and about the precious rabbit, I tried to take a step back and instead went tumbling backward in the snow. In another second the fox was upon me, on my chest, scrabbling to get at my shoulder, my neck. I felt a line of pain run up my skin, just between my neck and my shoulder over the collarbone. After all this I was going to be killed by a fox! What a bad, bad way to go.

I managed to roll over, so I was now on top of him, hoping my weight would crush him, but it only made his teeth sink in farther.

I couldn't think. Or at least, my thoughts weren't connected to my actions. I balled up my right hand into a fist and drove it crookedly into his side, knocking the breath out of him. Just for a second, but it was enough for me to snatch my knife, tucked deep in my coat pocket. I whipped it out and held it at my shoulder, feeling suddenly like a warrior, out for blood. When the fox lunged for me again, I was ready. Ready and waiting.

I cried the whole time I ate. I knew I shouldn't, but the warrior girl was gone, and I felt guilty for what I'd done—stealing a poor animal's food and killing him, too. I added it to my pile of guilt like I added logs to the fire that was now blazing in front of me. And I knew I would do it again. Now that I'd started, I was ready to become a hunter.

It didn't seem right that God made it a mortal sin to kill other people but didn't include killing any other creature, when animals of all sorts seemed to have cares just like the rest of us—families and homes and hunger and such. Well, I reasoned, I was just going to have to live with it. God wasn't fair. I was learning that lesson.

I stayed in that spot all the next day, drying the meat that was left. It wouldn't last me all that long, since the fox had been lean and the rabbit was already half eaten, but I needed the rest, anyway. The next morning I packed up the strips of meat in my bundled scarf and headed on my way.

It turned out I wasn't ready to become a hunter. Or rather, I wasn't able. I didn't see hide nor hair of another creature besides birds from that time onward. I was done with the dried meat in two days, and then it started to snow.

Keeping moving was the hardest. I had nowhere to shelter, no energy or time to build a lean-to, so there was no point in trying to wait out the winter storm. Instead I walked through it, hardly seeing anything, hardly knowing if I was still going in the right direction.

At night I didn't sleep—it was hard to keep my fire burning long enough to drift off, and my clothes were damp and cold all the way through, and I was getting a cough that racked my chest and kept me from any rest I might have had, curled up in a ball under a rocky overhang or stand of pine trees. I wondered about what the Reverend had said, about the poison making me want to sleep. Maybe I'd skipped right over the sleeping part and was now in the second stage, the sicker stage. How could I know?

Just like I can't describe the pain of losing Katie, I can't explain the misery of those days after the fox. I know it couldn't have been very long, but it felt like weeks. My dream of Boston had turned into a faded pinpoint in the distance. I would have turned and gone back the way I'd come, back to Lance King's shelter, but I'd come too far to make it back alive.

I wondered at my feelings, when I'd been back there at the

shelter, of wanting to die. Now I feared dying in these woods more than anything in the world, even living with Katie's death, even dying of poison months down the road. There was nothing beautiful to me about the woods anymore. Even if I could have seen more than a few feet in front of me, I wouldn't have welcomed the sight.

In my daze, the open field I walked across on that last day didn't mean anything to me. I didn't think of it as meaning that somebody must have cleared the land for farming . . . until I saw the barn, tall on the other side of a hedge of oak trees.

I wouldn't have thought I had the strength, but when I saw those wooden slats and the sloping roof and the big wooden entrance, I burst into a run. That barn meant shelter and warmth. I ran across the field, around the side of the barn, and crashed through the doors, the sweet scent of stale hay and of horses and leather hitting me all at once. I almost cried with happiness. They were such familiar smells, but it seemed like I hadn't smelled them in years.

Feeling like I could faint at any minute but not caring anymore, I took a look at my surroundings as I caught my breath. The barn was one large room with a loft built in about halfway up and stalls along one side. Green-brown hay was stacked in great piles in one corner, and along the walls hung all sorts of tack and farming equipment, all gray with dust. The horses that had obviously been here at one point were gone now. The barn had been used, but not in a while.

Pulling off my hat and mittens, I closed the door behind me and stumbled over to the hay, collapsing onto the nearest pile. I pulled handfuls of the thick strands around me, smelling them, feeling the thickness and dryness warming me down to my very bones. The deep breaths I took sent me into a coughing spasm, and I clamped my hand over my mouth. There might be a house nearby—this barn had to belong to someone. What if they heard me?

I forced myself to get up and scavenge around for something to eat. There was an old sack of horse feed and a couple of moldy, shriveled apples. Finally I came upon a couple of potatoes, discarded in a corner of the room. They were old and growing roots, but they were something. I tore off the roots and then bit into one, skin and all. Swallowing hurt my throat, and my belly protested against the food, maybe because it hadn't had anything inside it for so long or maybe because it knew moldy potatoes weren't any good for it. But I ate one of those raw potatoes in about two minutes flat—as fast as I could get it down. Then, amazingly full and sick to my stomach, I headed over to the hay.

I yanked off my wet coats and put them to the side to dry, then I settled in and pulled the hay all around me again. I even pulled it over my face, leaving enough room to breathe but not enough so anyone could see me if they came in. I didn't want anyone sneaking up on me in my sleep.

I stared up at the roof through the screen of hay, breathing in that sweet smell and remembering all the times I'd spent hiding in the stacks from Theo, back when we used to play hide-and-seek. It had taken him forever to catch on.

My body was going hot and cold, I guessed because of the change in temperature. Or maybe because I was scared. Or maybe I was sick, because of poison or cold or hunger or a million other reasons. But it didn't matter. I was warm now. I was safe.

CHAPTER TEN

Snuffle snuffle snuffle. Something was wet and slimy and noisy against my face. For a moment I thought it was Marlene, our striped cat, but then I remembered she was dead these two years. And then I remembered everything else.

Snuffle snuffle.

"Aaaahhhh!" I burst out of my cozy hay pile, swiping at my face and limbs. My back slammed against the wall as I looked around frantically to see where the critter had gone. As I did, the night before came back to me. I was in a barn. I'd gotten out of the cold. I was safe.

And now I could see that it wasn't a cat at all that had been rubbing against my face. It was a hound dog, and a puny-looking one at that. He stood a few feet away, watching me intensely, his tail wagging and his nose wiggling to catch my scent.

Phew. I let out a breath and sank to a crouch, reaching my hand out low and palm down.

"You scared the pants off me. Come here, boy."

The dog's tail started wagging double time, but his ears were laid back with fear. He inched toward me with a look that said he was ready to run at any moment. I half giggled, half coughed.

"I bet you make a real good hunting dog. Come here. I'm not going to hurt you." I waved my hand some more. I didn't stop to wonder if he might be a mean dog or if he might have a master trailing after him—I was too happy to see another face.

Slowly, delicately, his soft nose touched the very tip of my hand. He sniffed my knuckles, my fingers, then up along my arm. Then in another instant he leapt toward me, nearly knocking me over, and slobbered all over my face.

"Ha! Did I pass the test?" I returned the kisses by rubbing his floppy brown ears. I don't think I've ever been so happy to be slobbered on in all my life.

"Mookie! Get out here, girl!"

I gasped. My new friend, who I figured must be Mookie (and a girl at that), turned her head. The voice that was coming from outside—a loud, boy's voice—had startled both of us, and I immediately backed into the corner.

"Mookie!" The voice was getting closer.

My chest suddenly felt like someone was squeezing it. "Go on, get," I whispered, pushing on Mookie's behind to get her to move toward the door. Mookie looked at me once, scraggly tail still wagging. And then she started toward the voice, like a kid being called home to supper. Right before she walked out, she turned her big, brown, hopeful eyes on me—as if I might come along with her.

Not on your life, I thought. Mookie hung her head, like she could read the thought, and disappeared through the entrance.

I leaned back, feeling a mixture of fear and yearning. It had been so long since I'd heard a human voice. Part of me wanted to run right out there and throw my arms around that boy, whoever he was. But part of me—a deeper, more fearful part—said to hide. I tiptoed over to the far wall and peered through one of the slats, hoping to get a glimpse of him, but he and Mookie were nowhere to be seen. The snow had stopped, though.

For the first time in days the hunger in my gut didn't occupy all my mind. I was too busy thinking about that boy and what he might be like. The way the Reverend and Daddy always talked, people outside of Dogwood were almost like our enemies. The rare grown-ups who took a trip to the outside would come back with tales of things they'd heard—of murderers and kidnappers and such. Katie and I had always figured it was just the grown-ups trying to scare us to keep us in our place. But now the fear struck me: what if those stories were true? If there were really so many kidnappers and murderers out in the world, couldn't that boy be one of them?

"All right, Glory," I said to myself. "You're going to be smart about this. You're not going to be reckless." I pushed the vision of Katie that rose up sharply to the back of my mind. I'd learned my lesson.

* * *

By afternoon I'd decided to scout out the boy's house. I could look at him and his family and figure out if they were murderers or not. (How I'd figure that out I wasn't sure, but I guessed I'd come up with something.) If they seemed like good people, maybe I'd knock on their door and ask them for some food. If not—well, maybe I'd sneak into their house while they were sleeping and steal some food. Was it still a sin to steal, even if you were stealing from bad people? I wondered. Would God forgive you? But then I remembered that God and me weren't friends anymore and that I was the one who'd be doing any forgiving.

It wasn't as easy to find the boy's house as I'd expected, which was a relief. It made me feel safer to know I was camped out so far away.

At dusk I set off following Mookie's trail—which soon joined up with a pair of boot prints. The tracks stretched across clear rolling hills and through a tiny pine forest—but then they disappeared across a frozen pond, and I couldn't pick them up again on the other side. Finally, when I was about ready to cry with frustration, the smell of chimney smoke tickled at my nostrils and led me to the house.

It was big and white, whiter than any white I'd ever seen, and had two stories and a pretty little balcony jutting out of the second floor. It took my breath away because it was even fancier than the Johansens' place, and as I got closer up, I realized it was much bigger, too.

On the front porch sat two rocking chairs, to the left of a door with triangular windows cut out at the top. I wove closer and closer, keeping an eye out for the slightest movement that might mean somebody was coming in or out.

A road, lightly outlined in snow, led up to a shed that sat in a patch of pines beside the front corner of the house. That's where I headed, taking cover underneath the snow-powdered limbs, creeping ever closer to the nearest window. The moon was bright above me, reflecting off the snow. *Maybe I should come back later, when the moon is down. There'd be less chance of getting caught,* I thought. *I should head back to that pond and try to catch some fish.* It was a good idea, and my stomach certainly seemed to agree. I felt like I might faint from hunger. But I needed at least a glimpse of another human being more than anything right now.

Anyway, if there was one thing I was good at, it was spying. I wouldn't get caught.

From the closest pine tree to the nearest window it was about twenty feet. I held my breath and half tiptoed, half ran the distance, pulling myself flat against the house wall once I'd reached it.

Behind me, my footprints dotted the snow as clear as day. *Oh.* I hadn't even thought of leaving tracks. Well, too late now.

Slowly, quietly, I slid over to the corner of the window-pane. I could hear a soft murmur coming from inside and see something cooking, which made my mouth water and my stomach growl. Hoping that somebody wasn't looking out the window at that very moment and planning to run if they were, I peered in through the glass.

The view was like nothing I'd ever seen.

I'd happened to choose the kitchen window, and I don't think there could have been a more amazing room in the whole house. The floor was covered in a shiny material decorated in swirling yellow patterns. The stove didn't seem like a stove at all—it was big and square, with a window in the front and four coiling eyes on top. Through the window I could see right into the oven, where a cake was baking in a round pan.

And the lights. I'd heard of electric lights before, but I'd never imagined them to be so bright. The room was glowing like a million lit candles.

Through the kitchen door, which was wide and arched, I could see a small wooden table. Sitting at the table were a man, a woman, and a boy. A family, having supper together—the same as folks back home. The mother was holding a dish in one hand and scooping green beans from it onto her plate. Her hair was shorter than I'd ever seen on a woman, and she was wearing pants and a button-down shirt just like a man. The man, the father, was reaching across the table for a little glass jar with a shiny silver top. It was filled with something white. Salt, I guessed, as I watched him sprinkle it on his plate.

The meal spread out before them, too, was like nothing I'd

ever seen. There was a big glass tray brimming with red sauce, and below, through the glass, I could see layers of cheese, and meat, and what looked like noodles. It looked so good, I felt like I could taste it. The green beans, an everyday food in Dogwood, looked exotic in their own glass bowl, topped with what appeared to be chopped nuts. What I wouldn't have done for just a bite! And still there was a third bowl, of lettuce and chopped tomatoes and carrots—lettuce leaf salad, in the dead of winter!

I finally tore my eyes away from the food for a moment to look at the boy, the third member of the family. He looked two or three years older than me, about Theo's age maybe, with a smattering of freckles on his nose and short, dirty blond hair. He was digging into his meal, his long skinny body hunched over the plate. Every once in a while he took a large, greedy swig from his milk glass before lifting another forkful of food to his mouth. He didn't look anything like Theo, but he reminded me of him all the same.

My mouth must have dropped open because the scene was taking on a cloudy look, and I realized I'd been breathing mist on the glass. I rubbed it away carefully and continued to stare at the family before me. I didn't notice that I'd roused Mookie until two paws appeared with a tap on the windowsill before me, followed by two ears standing on alert and a pair of big brown eyes. I jerked back from the window and pressed myself against the wall, sucking in so much air that I almost went into a coughing fit, which I muffled by putting a hand over my mouth.

Woof, woof, woof!

Drat it! I kept still, hoping Mookie would forget about me.

Woof!

I cringed as I heard the sound of a chair being pushed back from the table and, a moment later, a door behind the house creaking open.

"Go on, Mookie. Just come back sometime tonight, you hear?" It was the boy's voice. I could hear Mookie's claws tap-tapping across the porch and then crunching into the snow.

Without waiting a moment longer, I burst into a run. It was a foolish thing to do, I know. Mookie was a hound dog, for heaven's sake, and of course she'd be able to catch up to me in no time flat. But even though the boy and his family didn't look like murderers, I wasn't, I just was *not* ready to be found.

I was halfway over the first rise when I looked down and saw Mookie was already at my side. She wasn't barking or try-ing to catch me—she was just running beside me, her tongue lolling out to the side, a goofy dog smile on her face as if we were playing some kind of game.

I slowed down with relief, panting, and offered her a pat on the head. "All right," I said. "All right."

Once we were far enough away from the house that I didn't feel in danger anymore, I came to a standstill. The sky had opened up to let down a light mist of snow, which I realized thankfully would cover my tracks, at least a little bit. The fields were hushed, and it suddenly struck me how happy I was to be seeing fields and not the same thick woods and craggy rocks and endless sameness.

"All right," I said again, my stomach punctuating the word with a loud groan. I crouched down to eye level with Mookie, pulling her face toward me and rubbing my cold nose against hers. "I'll talk to them tomorrow. Now let's go catch some fish."

Mookie didn't say a word.

The next day went on a lot like that first one. Fishing had proved to be easy enough—and of course, eating my catch had been heavenly. Finding a place to build a fire out of sight had been harder, but I'd built it small enough that it wouldn't be seen. So I did it all again in the morning—fished, cooked, ate. Then I went exploring the fields until dusk, though I don't know what I expected to find. I told myself it was to learn more about the folks that lived here, but really, I think I was just stalling, putting off the moment when I would have to approach them.

They were farmers, that was for sure—they had lots of cows and lots of land, with another barn about a quarter mile behind the house. I didn't see where they were getting their vegetables from or the other supplies I'd glimpsed through their kitchen window—boxes and cans with colorful labels, containing heaven only knew what.

Spying that night, I was careful not to catch Mookie's

attention again. I couldn't bring myself to knock on the door. I didn't know when I'd be ready. Mrs. Johansen used to say it was nothing big in a place like Boston to say hello to someone you'd never met, but I just couldn't imagine walking up to those folks and introducing myself when I'd never introduced myself to anyone in my entire life.

Still, I longed to know them. In fact, maybe it's crazy, but as I watched through the window, I pretended they were members of my own family. I had a sudden image of them adopting me, and I imagined the boy's name just happening to be Theo, and I imagined calling his folks Mama and Daddy. I knew it was disloyal to my own family to even think like this, but then, to my own family, I didn't even exist anymore. And this family wouldn't know about all the bad stuff I'd done. They'd love me just as if I'd never done anything terrible. And when I died, they'd cry over me and bury me in the cemetery out back. I'd have an angelic look on my face and they'd say just that—that I was an angel on earth, and it was such a shame that I'd died at such a young age, but maybe God wanted me back in heaven with him. And they'd pray for me.

Of course, that wasn't real life. Real life was me getting to Boston. And dying, and being buried . . . Ugh. I would think on that more later, after I'd made it. But to make it, I needed this family's help.

Still, what if they *were* bad people? Or worse, what if they could see through me and realize I was a bad person? What if they refused to help me because they could see how bad I was?

It was with these thoughts that I turned in for the night. They spun in circles around my head while I lay awake in my nest of hay and wove themselves into my dreams long after that, when my head was filled with visions of home, and Katie, and endless hungry walking through the woods alone.

When I heard the footsteps in the barn, I thought at first that they were my own dream footsteps, crunching leaves and branches and snow on their long journey through the woods. I didn't understand that they were real until someone started turning the hay where I lay, buried out of sight.

Oh, God. Oh, God, I thought, now fully, painfully awake. My mouth was dry, my heart was beating in my ears. I hadn't stolen anything, but I felt as guilty as a thief about to be caught and just as scared, for I didn't know what my captors would do once they found me.

Why hadn't I thought they'd be in to turn the hay? Why had I figured a family would have a barn but never, ever use it? Stupid, stupid, stupid.

Scrunch. Scrunch. Scrunch.

I pulled my body in as tight as I could. Through the screen of hay, I could see a figure moving back and forth, but I couldn't tell who it was. Should I run? Should I just stay put and hope they went away? How bad would it hurt to get stabbed by a pitchfork?

That last thought made up my mind for me. I burst out of the hay, racing for the barn door. In a blur I saw that the path was clear in front of me, and if I didn't dare look behind me, I might just make it out in one piece. My legs moved, my arms pumped. I slammed both hands onto the long planks of the door and pushed. . . .

And felt a hand grab the back of my coat. The figure wedged itself between me and the door, so that the sun poured in behind . . . him, it was a him. I saw the outline of his tall form. And then the ground came tilting toward me.

CHAPTER
ELEVEN

I tried to lift my head, but it felt like it was filled with water.

"Just relax," a voice said. My eyelids fluttered open. The face before me was not my daddy's. It was the face of the boy from the house—first fuzzy and far away, then clearer—so clear, I could see each individual freckle on his nose.

"Theo," I said, knowing he wasn't Theo, but somehow thinking the name I'd given him in my imagination was the right one.

"I'm Jacob. Jake," he replied. "You fainted. You're okay."

"Jake," I repeated. I felt cozy and cared for, and I nestled into the warmth that was all around me, happy. Then I noticed that the softness and warmth my head was resting on was the crook of his arm. And I remembered he was a stranger.

"Umph!" I shoved him away and rolled out of his arms, coming to rest on my knees a few feet away. Jake leapt to his feet, and as I made a dash for the barn door again, he swung his arms wide, blocking my way.

"Shhh!" he said. "It's all right. I'm not going to hurt you! Please!"

I didn't have much of a choice. I stopped. He was blocking

the door and besides, where was I going to go? Back into the woods? My legs went wobbly at the thought, and I slumped down onto the floor.

Jake inched toward me slowly, as if I were a wild animal, and then sat down a few feet away. I realized then, looking him up and down, that I must *look* like a wild animal—my hair all tangled and matted and full of hay, my face all dirty. His clothes were clean and neat—dungarees, work boots, a leather coat smoother than any I'd seen. I shuddered to think what I must smell like. In all my worrying about food and shelter, I'd forgotten to even long for a bath.

"I . . . I . . ." I wanted to explain everything, how I'd ended up in his barn and how I wasn't stealing or anything, just trying to sleep someplace warm, and I wanted to ask him not to hurt me, but the words just wouldn't come out. How much could I tell him? How much had he guessed?

"Are you a runaway?" he asked, breaking the silence for me. I had to think for a minute to figure out what he was saying.

"Did you run away from home?"

"Uh." I cleared my throat. "No. Um, I was lost in the woods, and I . . . I saw your barn and I decided to just sleep here for the night. I'm sorry. . . ."

"For the night?" he said, looking at the pile of things he'd exposed when he'd unearthed me—my mug, my knife, my second coat, a pile of kindling.

"Well, for a couple of nights. A few nights."

Jake studied me closely, with an expression that I couldn't quite understand. Now that he was beside me, I realized he didn't look at all like Theo. He was handsome, for one. And right away it was clear he was from a different set of people than the folks in Dogwood, who—besides the Johansens—are mostly dark haired, with tan skin (some say it's on account of Indian ancestors, which I only half believe). Jake's eyes were almost the color of the hay I'd been sleeping under. His skin was pale against the freckles.

I decided right then and there that he wasn't scary at all. I don't know why; it was just something deep inside that told me I didn't need to be afraid.

"You don't want to tell me if you're a runaway or not." He said it like a statement, but it was more of a question.

I opened my mouth to say it wasn't what he thought, but instead I just closed it and shook my head. If I told about being sent out of Dogwood, I'd have to tell about why. And on top of that, I was feeling too shy to talk—otherwise I would have just burst with words about how happy I was to see another human being and one who wasn't scary and what a horrible time I'd had in the woods.

Jake stared at me hard for another long minute. Then he seemed to make up his mind. "Well, you seem harmless enough."

Me, harmless? I almost laughed. *He* was the stranger, not me.

He paused and looked me over again. "Whoa, this is just like a movie." I couldn't think of anything to say to that.

Jake looked at me, then at the barn door, then back at me. "Don't worry. I won't tell."

"Tell what?" I asked.

"Tell my parents that you're here. It can be our secret."

I hadn't even thought of Jake's parents until that moment. "W-would they be mad?"

"Well, not exactly. But, you know, they'd probably want to call the authorities if you're a—for being a young girl out on her own and stuff. But don't worry, I'm not going to let that happen." He puffed out his chest a bit as he said this.

"The authorities?"

"You know, the cops."

"Cops?"

"The police. You know, if you're under eighteen and you've run away. They take runaways and either bring them back to their parents or bring them to jail. Don't you know that?"

Cops? Runaways? Jail? I had only a vague idea of what this all meant. Police were people who could arrest you if you did something against the law. My daddy hated police. And now here was this boy telling me they could catch me just on account of thinking I might be a *runaway*, something Jake obviously believed me to be.

"I don't have parents," I said, panicked.

Jake's eyes widened.

"I don't. I really don't. I don't have a family. I—I didn't run away."

I could tell he only half believed me by the way one of his eyebrows went up, but it was in a friendly kind of way, like if I *was* lying, he wouldn't get mad.

"Well, where did you come from, then?"

"I can't tell," I said, sucking in my breath. "I mean, it doesn't matter because I can't go back there, and I . . ." I tried to think back to the lines I'd made up in my head for when I met the folks in the house, but I couldn't remember them. "I need your help. I just need to get to the nearest town. But if you don't want to help me because the . . . the cops'll get you or something, that's okay. Maybe you could just tell me which way to walk and I'll leave you alone and—"

"Hold on! Slow down." Jake inched forward. "I'm not worried about the cops getting me—that's crazy. Maybe you don't want to tell me where you're from, but one thing's for sure. You're not walking from here to town. The nearest *real* town is almost two hours' drive away, and . . . well, look at you." He took in my whole figure in a glance. "You look pretty sick, if you don't mind me saying. Half starved, too. Where in the world have you been?"

I didn't answer. I just looked down at my own body. I remembered sitting in the woods and circling my wrist with my fingers. Since then my skin had taken on a whitish, transparent color, and my veins stood out blue and clear. I moved my hands up to my ribs and realized that yes, they did stick out a lot more than I ever remembered.

"What would you do when you got to town, anyway?" Jake pressed. "Do you have any money? What're you going to eat? Are you planning to see someone when you get there? Because you can use my phone and have them come get you."

I shook my head, helpless. How far of a walk was a two-hour drive? How was I going to get to Boston if it wasn't through towns? Walking the whole way, I realized, would be impossible.

"Look, you can stay here tonight. I'll bring you leftovers from dinner—my mom won't even notice. But then tomorrow we'll call your parents, okay? Or if you really don't have parents like you say, we'll call whoever is supposed to take care of you. 'Cause otherwise you're going to get yourself thrown in jail, or die of starvation, or even worse. Now just say yes."

My bottom lip began to tremble. I looked down at my hands to hide my tearing eyes. "I can't," I whispered, hardly loud enough for Jake to hear. "I don't have anyone. I swear."

Jake clearly didn't know what to make of me. His shoulders heaved up and down once. "Hey, I'm sorry. Hey." He moved his hand to my arm and gave me an awkward pat, moving in a bit closer. "Please, I'm sorry."

I swiped at my eyes and tried my best at a smile. "No, it's okay. Maybe I could just stay here tonight and then tomorrow, um, tomorrow I'll just head to . . ." Where? What was I going to do? Where was I going to go? Did it matter? If it was impossible to get to the nearest town, it was unthinkable that I'd make it to Boston.

"Wait," Jake said. He pressed his hand harder against my arm. "Look, maybe we can figure something out. At least stay here tonight so I can give you a couple of good meals. And . . ." I could tell he was struggling with a decision. "And I'll do what I can. I mean, I don't have a car or anything, but maybe my dad's—well, we'll figure something out. If you really are all alone, we'll figure it out. Okay?"

I tried to gauge Jake's honesty by his eyes, which Daddy said were the only way to tell. They looked warm and free of guilt, which was probably more than I could say for mine. I tried to smile, and this time it came easier. "Okay," I said.

"Okay," he said. There were lots of *okays* going all around.

"Hey," he said suddenly. "You haven't told me your name yet."

I thought about whether I could really trust this stranger or not, and I thought about making something up. I thought this was my chance to give myself a new name since my old life was long gone—a new name for whatever life I had left. Then I thought about my name being part of who I was, for better or for worse, whether I liked it or not.

"Glory," I said, stretching out my hand to shake his. "My name is Glory Mason."

Jake didn't talk at all like the folks at home. He didn't call his folks Mama and Daddy, he didn't say things like, "I reckon." Most of all his voice didn't tilt and rise and dip in the same way folks' did back home, and his words were short and clipped, rather than long and drawn out and slow. Jake laughed when I remarked on this. And then he said that my accent took the cake.

I didn't stay one night, like we'd talked about. I stayed several. But given the way things had been going lately, that wasn't any surprise. This whole journey seemed to be taking a lot longer than I'd ever dreamed—I wasn't even out of the woods yet, really.

Since meeting Jake, though, I felt much better inside and out. My body was getting back to normal. Jake brought me things to wash with—even buckets of hot water here and there—and a toothbrush and toothpaste. He sneaked me three square meals a day, breakfast, lunch, and dinner, when he was supposed to be out doing chores. Plus snacks like cookies and this kind of cold crispy cereal that he brought in a bowl with milk, and that was divine. Half the food he said his mama hadn't even made—it came from either a box or a can—and unbelievably, it was all delicious, too. I hadn't even eaten this much in Dogwood. Jake teased me that he was fattening me up for Thanksgiving dinner next year.

At first I stiffened right up, remembering what everyone in Dogwood always said about outsiders. Then I noticed the look in Jake's eyes, and I laughed at my foolishness. "You know, you aren't so different from the folks back home," I said, thinking of Theo's sense of humor.

"What home is that, Glory?" Jake asked. My mouth shut like a trap until he changed the subject. Jake knew I couldn't give him an answer.

Mostly he was respectful about not asking me too many questions, even though I was sure he'd already figured out a lot more than I wanted him to. He knew that I was from a town not too far away. He knew something bad had happened there, but he didn't know what.

I appreciated that he let me keep the most important secrets to myself. He could have forced me to tell, seeing as he was the only thing standing between me and starvation. But it was clear that even though he knew there were things I wasn't saying, he believed I was honest and trusted me enough to keep me in his family's barn, a secret from everyone.

Deep down, I knew I didn't deserve that trust. But I couldn't help craving it and longing to keep it. Jake was my friend. I'd started caring about him, and selfish as it was, undeserving as I was, I wanted him to stay my friend. My only one in the whole world.

Well, I guess there was Mookie, too. She was a constant third in our meetings. She'd follow Jake out when he brought the meals and check on me every once in a while on her own, giving my face a quick lick or a wet nose print before traipsing off. At night, which was the time that Jake stayed with me for a while to talk, Mookie would lie between us on the hay, snoring.

During these times I asked Jake a lot about his parents and his home. Were his folks as nice as I imagined them to be? Did his mama wear perfume? Where'd they get their clothes? I had to be subtle about it, 'cause if I asked him too many questions about modern doodads and such he would realize how out of place I really was, and then he might know I was from Dogwood. From all I knew, Dogwood was one of a kind, especially by Mrs. Johansen's accounts and by the Reverend's constant sermons on how "special" and "chosen" we were. We were *specially* backward, I was almost certain.

And if Jake figured out where I was from, there was still a sliver of a chance that he, thinking he was doing good, would try to get me back to Dogwood. And that would be a disaster.

So I tried to keep as much to myself as possible, and he asked very few questions. It was like there was this unsaid bargain between us that for the time we spent together, as short as it promised to be, we wouldn't talk about my history. We'd pretend I didn't have one, and we'd just talk about the future instead. With me and Jake, at least, there'd be no looking back.

CHAPTER
TWELVE

Jake broke our bargain that Wednesday. I knew it was Wednesday, and January 20, too, because he'd told me so.

I'd been making a log of all the food he'd been giving me, with a pencil and paper he'd given me, so I could pay him back someday. I'd asked him what the date was so I could put it at the top, and that was when he told me. I couldn't believe I'd been out here—in the woods or sleeping in a barn for that long! But then, it seemed like it'd been so much longer.

"I don't know why you're making that crazy log, anyway," Jake said. "It's all just leftovers."

"I don't want charity, that's all," I said. "In—where I'm from, we aren't raised to take charity."

Jake stopped what he was doing and looked at me, his green eyes peering seriously into mine. I dropped my hands to my sides, nervous.

"It's no use, Glory. I know where you're from."

I sat still as a statue. I couldn't think of one word to say.

"You're from Dogwood."

"Uh," I breathed, feeling like the wind had been knocked

out of me. "No, you're wrong. I've never—"

"It's no use, Glory. That's the only town it could be, now that I've really thought about it. I figured it out last night. It's the only one close enough—over by Mineral Caverns, right? Where all the religious . . . folks live. I guess it's not really a town, more of an outpost or something like that. I'm right, aren't I?"

"Not a town?"

"Glory. I'm right, aren't I?"

I hung my head and rubbed my eyes. Suddenly I was so, so tired. I nodded.

Jake's eyebrows leapt near the top of his forehead, like suddenly he was just too curious to hold it in. "What happened, Glory? What's it like there? Why'd you leave? You've gotta tell me. I promise I won't tell *anyone.*"

"Well, I . . . it's a long story. I—"

"Don't worry. I won't try to make you go back."

I hadn't realized I'd been holding my breath until he said those words. All the fear just drained out of my body. Of course. Of course Jake wouldn't try to make me go back and face the people who'd cast me out. He was a true friend, and he obviously thought I'd left Dogwood of my own accord.

"Was it the weird ritual stuff?" he continued. "I've heard they're just crazy over there. Bible bangers and fanatics and stuff. Did they make you—"

"Fanatics? Bible bangers?" I repeated the words. I had no

idea what they meant. But I could tell they weren't good.

"They didn't make you worship snakes, did they?"

The blood was rushing to my head so fast, I could feel my cheeks going red. What was he talking about?

"Or sacrifice babies or anything like that?"

That was the last straw. I jumped up. "Sacrifice *babies?* Are you crazy? You wouldn't know the first thing about it, and you can just keep your mouth shut!"

I had time to notice Jake's stunned expression as I stormed to the opposite end of the barn. Fanatics! Bible bangers! Worshiping snakes? So that's what the outside world thought about us? I began to snatch up my things. I had no more items than the day I'd left my shelter outside of Dogwood, and I was able to shove everything into my scarf/sack in ten seconds flat. I was just out the barn door when Jake grabbed the back of my coat.

"Glory, wait."

"Leave me alone," I said, shoving him away, almost punching him in my rage.

"Glory, I'm sorry. I didn't know!"

"You're right! You don't know anything about my family, or Dogwood, or . . . or anything!" I spun around.

Jake looked stunned and even a little scared, but he didn't budge. We stood there staring at each other, second after second. Whatever he was going to say, I was going to defend myself—with words or even my fists.

And then he poked his chin out. "Hit me if you want to," he said. "I deserve it."

I hadn't been expecting *that*. I looked down at my hands and realized I'd been unconsciously clenching them into fists.

Looking back up, I saw that Jake's mouth was down-turned in concern, and his freckles had disappeared because his skin was flushed red. "If you had any idea how sorry I was, though, you wouldn't."

I looked at him for another second. Oh. Oh, Lord. I was making too much of this. He hadn't meant it. He just didn't know any better. And after all he'd done for me. And who would have thought I'd ever be defending my town like this? Did I have to be so sensitive? It was just him talking about Dogwood that way, and me missing it so much, and . . .

I shifted from foot to foot. I plucked at my thumbnail. Then I gave Jake my best attempt at a grin, which felt more like a grimace.

"If you knew how hard I could hit, you'd run in the other direction," I said.

He stayed still for a moment longer, like he wasn't sure if I was joking or not. And then he snorted. And the snort turned into a laugh. And pretty soon I was laughing, too.

That evening Jake appeared at the barn door with something besides food.

"It's a magazine," he said. "My mom has a subscription. She gets one every month."

I wanted to devour those pages right then and there, but Jake said he figured I wasn't going to be able to put the magazine down once I picked it up, so I'd better eat first.

After supper we hunkered down in the hay—me on my stomach, Jake sitting up against the barn wall. He held the magazine in his hands. But when I reached for it, he pulled it away, ever so slightly.

"First I want to know something."

I pulled back. "Okay."

"Glory, where are you going? I mean, to the nearest town, but then where, to do what?"

I fiddled with my fingernails. I didn't know why I hadn't told this to him yet, but somehow Boston seemed so far away that maybe I thought he would laugh. Or worse, tell me it was impossible. They weren't the best reasons. And Jake deserved to know. He was helping me get there.

"Boston. I'm going to Boston."

Jake's brow furrowed. His face seemed precious to me— kind and concerned.

"Do you have family there?"

"No. No, I don't know a soul there," I said, pausing a minute, seeing he needed more of an answer. "I . . . well, it'll sound really silly, I guess, but I promised someone I'd go there."

"Who?"

"My friend."

"Why does your friend care whether you go to Boston or not?"

Him talking about Katie as if she were still in the present and not the past made my heart clench up. I gathered myself. "Was that one question or thirty you wanted to ask? I have to get there, that's all. No two ways about it."

"Okay, okay," Jake said, raising up his free hand as if to stop me. "I gotcha. It's a long way, though."

I nodded. "Jake? I have a question for you."

"Shoot," he said.

"Why are you helping me? Why do you care?"

Jake's breath whooshed out of his mouth as he raised his hands and rested them behind his head. "Boredom, mostly." He laughed.

I just stared. I really wanted to know.

"Okay, well, maybe boredom really is a tiny part of it. Or it was," he said, turning earnest. "It seemed like something you'd see on TV, finding a strange girl hiding out in your barn." He smiled, a bit apologetically. "Things aren't too exciting around here for me, you know? The life of a farmer's son, only child and all . . ."

He didn't stop to see if I agreed or understood. "But now I know you, and I can't help caring. I feel *bad* for you. I try to put myself in your shoes—all alone, cold and hungry—and I can't even imagine how you've made it this far. You're just the toughest, most determined person I've met. I guess I admire you, too."

He paused another second. I could feel myself blushing. As absurd as having somebody admire me seemed, I still couldn't help feeling flattered.

"Ah-hmm." Jake cleared his throat, adjusting himself in his place against the wall. "Anyways . . ."

He lifted up the magazine, as if to draw my attention back to the reason we were really sitting here. He flipped open the first page. Then he began to show me a tiny glimpse into what I'd been missing all my life.

The magazine was like a book, only skinnier, and glossy and full of photographs. There were beautiful girls in makeup and clothes made out of fabrics I could never have imagined. There were movie stars—and I could see why people called them that because everything about them was light and glowing—walking down red carpets, hugging each other, laughing. There were little stories—Jake called them articles—that talked about things like women and their jobs and women and their babies and how such and such survived such and such ordeal. Everybody looked so happy—everybody was smiling for the camera. I figured they all must be rich because they were all wearing such fancy clothes and they all looked so clean, with beauty shop haircuts and all.

The best was the perfume page. It was this page somewhere near the middle where you opened up this little sticky flap and rubbed the paper on your wrist. It smelled divine.

The more excited I got, the bigger Jake smiled. Now that he knew my secret—well, part of it, anyway—I could ask him all the questions I wanted, and he seemed to be happy answering them. *No, Glory, that's a dog. I know it doesn't look real; it's called a poodle. You're right, there's no such thing as aliens, it's just special effects for the movies. Special effects is when they use computers to make things happen in movies when they can't happen in real life.*

It all made my head spin. Each answer brought up new questions—like how did a computer work and what exactly could it do? I begged Jake to bring me more magazines. I asked him if he could sneak the TV out to the barn.

"Well, first of all, you'd need to plug it in," he said, laughing, his floppy hair bouncing with every *ha*. "There's no place to do that in the barn. But you know, Glory, you should also try to take it easy. I mean, it's a lot to take in, isn't it? I dunno, you tell me."

I considered. Maybe he was right. All this was so strange and exciting, but also scary. Maybe I just ought to take it one step at a time. Hopefully I'd get to see it all on my own soon enough.

Jake and I hadn't forgotten for one minute to think about how we were going to get to Shadow Tree, the town he had told me about. Or at least, I hadn't forgotten. Jake said he didn't have a driver's license (even though he knew how to drive 'cause his dad let him haul firewood and things like that), so his folks would never allow him to take a trip to Shadow Tree alone. We'd discussed telling them about me but figured it was too risky. They might well call the Child Welfare Protection Agency, thinking it was the best thing for me to be sent back home.

In the end, we decided we'd just have to wait till an opportunity came along. Jake's family had not one but *two* cars, and he said that sometimes his folks went to visit his aunt and slept over, especially now because she was pregnant and didn't have a husband, and his mom insisted on his dad taking her over there to help out (because Jake's mom didn't like driving in the snow), and that the next time they went, we could make our move.

I waited for that day eagerly, even though I couldn't imagine a boy like Jake knowing how to drive a car, not to mention drive one safely. I had visions of us crashing or getting caught by the police. As much as I wanted to find out what it was like to ride in a car, it seemed like it must be one of the most dangerous things in the world.

Over the next few days Jake did bring me some more magazines, which always filled me with pleasure. And as he revealed more and more about the outside world to me, he asked more and more questions about home. He couldn't believe that we had no electricity, or that I'd never been outside of the town, or that we grew all our own food and made just about all of our clothes, or that we didn't use money.

"Wow. And I thought *my* family was out of touch. No offense."

I shrugged. I knew he didn't mean it badly.

"It's just, my family lives out here in the woods, but I go to school, and we have so many things that connect us to the rest of the world."

At the mention of school, I felt sad. Jake was on vacation right now, and he'd had plenty of time to spend with me, without having to make up too many stories for his parents. He said he just told them he was out playing with Mookie. But soon his school would start back up again, and he wouldn't be around to keep me company. It was looking more and more like I wasn't going to be gone before then.

"But folks are nice in Dogwood? I mean, you don't talk about it like it was a bad place."

"Oh, no, it's a good place," I said. "Everybody looks out for each other, and everybody's like family. There aren't any police because nobody gets in trouble (*besides me*, I thought), and nobody is allowed to go without, and . . ."

I went on and on about home, glad to have the chance to share it with someone else. My homesickness had never left me for a second, and it felt good to let it out. Jake listened thoughtfully and seemed to really care about this and that little detail, like how I taught school and what the kids were like and how my granddaddy sometimes carved us toys out of bits of wood.

I was careful not to talk about Katie. Whenever she made her way into a story, which happened a lot, I just called her "my friend" and moved on. Jake didn't seem to notice. I felt disloyal somehow doing that, but I knew that if I talked about her too much or used her name, my feelings about what had happened would show.

I also didn't talk about God and how everyone in Dogwood made Him a part of every little thing they did. I didn't want to give Jake the wrong impression, that folks at home were just crazy and obsessed with being Christians. And then, I had my own doubts about God and what I'd always been taught about Him. How would I ever be able to explain it all to someone else?

So Jake and I continued our chats, staying off certain topics, and continued making our plans. Then one night, after I'd finished a dinner of beef stew and rice, he told me that his parents were going away Friday morning to stay with his aunt for the weekend. That was only three days away. And that was when we were going to make our move.

CHAPTER
THIRTEEN

"Glory, I have something to ask you," Jake said. "Another something."

"Okay."

"I don't think you'll want to answer this one."

"Well, we'll see."

"But I really need to ask it."

"Okay."

Jake and Mookie and I were sitting by the fire in the woods behind the barn. It was the night before the morning his parents were to go on their visit. We were going to leave the following evening, after dark, so there'd be less chance of being seen by the police.

"Why'd you leave Dogwood? Really?"

I choked on the piece of meat, a hot dog, I had in my mouth, and started coughing. Jake patted me on the back.

Why was I surprised? I should have been surprised he hadn't asked the question before now.

My coughing fit subsided, and I took a deep breath. It struck me that I hadn't had a coughing fit in a long time. I never felt dizzy anymore. My ribs had started disappearing under a healthier weight. I had Jake to thank for that.

It was almost possible to believe the poison in me from drinking the Water of Judgment didn't exist or that it wasn't working the way it was supposed to. It wasn't true, but it was a nice daydream.

Jake continued. "Because I've been thinking a lot, you know, about this thing we're going to do. About taking you to town and all."

I nodded cautiously.

"And it just seems like a big adjustment to me. It seems like too much. I mean, Glory, really, how are you going to make money once you get there? People are sure to notice a young girl on her own. You have to be sixteen to get a real job. And what about a place to live?"

We'd talked about all this before, in very vague details. Jake had decided on Shadow Tree as the town for me because it was close enough, and big enough to offer some opportunities for making money, but not so big that I'd be lost in it. And we'd figured I could just camp on the outskirts of town. There was a place he said might work, even though he worried it might be dangerous.

But the specifics, I guess I'd been too scared to get into those.

"And that's not even the biggest thing," Jake continued. "Glory, I just don't know how town life, or especially Boston life, is going to affect you. I mean, the way you talk about Dogwood, it's like everybody is good and trustworthy, and there aren't any modern conveniences, and I'm worried . . . I'm just worried the world is going to swallow you up."

I stared into the fire, poking it with my hot dog stick. I knew Jake was right to worry. But he didn't understand that I had no other choice. And he certainly didn't understand that my days were numbered and that the world was going to swallow me up no matter what—swallow me into a grave—and this was my one chance to do something before that happened.

I didn't know where to begin. I didn't know what to say and what to keep to myself. I started like this:

"I understand what you're trying to say. And I feel lucky that you care at all what happens to me. But . . . you just don't know. . . . I'm sick. Not just sick from being in the woods too long. I mean—I'm not going to get better."

Jake seemed to be drilling a hole in me with his stare. I continued.

"I can't go back home. I—I wish I could. But I did something bad. Really, really bad. So I can't go back. My friend Katie . . . she . . ." I paused to swallow the lump in my throat. "I promised her I would get to Boston. It's the only thing that I have now, do you know what I mean?"

I knew he couldn't possibly, but Jake nodded, anyway.

"I've got to get there. Really, please believe me, I just do. I—"

"It's okay, Glory. I don't understand, but I also sort of do." He looked up toward the sky, and I followed his gaze. All I could see were the eaves of the barn that sheltered our fire pit. "But you know, I'm sure whatever you did couldn't have been so bad. I'd still like you no matter what it was, if that's what you're worried about."

I choked out a laugh. Before leaving home, I'd never known laughter could be about anger and sadness and not about anything funny. "No," I said, shoving my stick into the dirt, which made it snap in half. "No. Believe me, you wouldn't."

That night I woke up to the feeling that someone was watching me from the darkness. My arms and neck crawled with gooseflesh. I could feel my blood pumping in my fingertips.

"Glory? Are you awake?"

I rolled over. "Jake?"

"My aunt's having the baby early," he whispered. "My mom and dad went to take her to the hospital. We've got to go now."

My pulse picked up, and a wave of nausea swept over me. I sat up in the darkness. "Why are you whispering?" I asked. Of all the questions I could have asked, that was the one that came out.

"I don't know," Jake said, his voice rising a few notches. "Here, I brought you these." He held out a bundle to me.

"Some of my mom's old clothes. She won't miss 'em. Here's the flashlight; I'll wait outside."

Jake went out of the barn into the moonlight, leaving me alone with my sick heart. Suddenly I didn't want to do this at all. Suddenly it was the thing I least wanted to do in all the world—to leave the safety of this barn, to say good-bye to Jake, the only friend I had, to go out into the big, wide, unknown world. Why had I been so excited about this? Why had I wanted it for so long? I couldn't imagine anything scarier.

The next few minutes I moved automatically. I made myself change out of my clothes and put on Jake's mama's clothes, which were loose but not as big on me as I'd expected. I made myself pick up my tin mug, my knife, and pack them into a knapsack Jake had given me. It was all happening so fast.

Suddenly I heard breathing right behind me, and just as I turned, I felt something slam into my side.

"Mookie!" I gasped. "Bad dog!" But I grabbed her around the neck and gave her a big bear hug. I was going to miss her a lot.

"Come on, girl," I said. "Let's go."

The night was clear. A thousand stars were twinkling, and the moon was glinting off the snow. Jake had gone to get the truck, so Mookie and I waited, one of us jittery with nerves. Aside from Mookie's slobbery dog sounds, the world was more silent than I could ever remember, and I strained my ears to hear the sound of a breeze, the cry of an owl, the rustle of dry branches.

Rrrruuuuoooom!

Every muscle inside me tensed. I knew that sound was Jake's daddy's truck. It was really happening! In another second or two, two white points of light came dancing across the field and then glared straight toward me. I hurried over to the place where I knew the road was dimly outlined in the snow.

The truck, growling and rumbling, pulled to a stop in front of me. The door on my side swung open, and a light flicked on inside the cab, showing me Jake—his hair messy from sleeping, circles under his eyes. His skin looked pale—but maybe that was just the kind of light it was.

He was doing all this for me. Just for me. I inwardly thanked God for him, forgetting for a second that God had let me down too much to be trusted anymore.

I climbed onto my seat. Mookie jumped in behind me and plopped down between Jake and me. And then we were on our way.

The truck roared and bounced down the road, following the tracks Jake's mother's car had made in the snow. As we rolled forward, Jake's eyes met mine expectantly—he was waiting to see what I would think about my first trip in a car. I laughed, breathless and, just for a second or two, as happy as I had ever been. I forgot about where I was going and why I was going and just laughed and laughed. I was in a real car—well, a truck, anyway. Me!

The road jostled and bounced us down a slope of mountain, sliding a little bit in the snow. The trees looked like black slashes through the window and moved faster and faster out of my view. The air was heavy with mist, and the patches of white floated toward us like ghosts. It reminded me of another night, one that felt like it had happened a million years ago.

"Better fasten your seat belt, Glory."

I struggled with the contraption he pointed to, not wanting to tear my eyes away from the world passing by us so quickly. Finally Jake had to help me fasten the metal part, closing it with a click.

All my tiredness and sickness of minutes before was gone. I noticed a familiar smell. Looking down to the right of the wheel Jake was steering with, I saw two mugs set in little holders, both steaming with the smell of coffee.

I hadn't had coffee in so long! I smiled at Jake gratefully and picked up the mug in both hands. The coffee tasted delicious, and the warm liquid seemed to penetrate every part of me.

Jake switched on the radio. He asked if I liked country music and I nodded, even though I didn't know if I'd ever heard it before. Probably not, since I'd only ever listened to a radio once before in my life. I was sure I *would* like it, no matter what, and it turned out I was right. The music twanged from hidden places all around us. I bobbed my head happily. Here I was in a truck, listening to the radio, with my new friend who had once been a stranger.

Glory Mason, I thought, *what is the world coming to?*

It was the kind of thought I would have had if none of the bad stuff that had happened had ever happened, and as if a big scary unknown weren't waiting ahead. It was a happy thought. I knew it couldn't last, but right now I didn't care. For the moment I just enjoyed it.

I turned my attention back to the window and didn't say a word for the rest of the ride.

CHAPTER
FOURTEEN

The clock said it was 5:13 A.M. when Jake said he needed to pull in for some gas. We were almost to Shadow Tree—we'd seen two signs for it already—along the wide, snow-cleared road we'd pulled onto soon after we'd left Jake's house. The bright lights of the gas station were the first signs of the outside world I had seen yet—we hadn't passed a car the entire time.

As we drove into the station, a *ding ding* sounded below us. Jake hopped out of the car, fiddled with the big metal box that gave out gas, and then came around to my side and opened my door.

"Well, we might as well load up while we're here," he said. "Come on, Glory, I'm going to take you into your very first store."

He had to tug my sleeve to get me to budge, but sure enough, he was soon pulling me into the well-lit space inside the station. Mookie perked up behind us, and I caught a glimpse of her mournful face, her nose pressed against the glass, as she jealously watched us enter the building.

Inside it was somehow even brighter than day, and there were shelves everywhere, with all kinds of food in colorful packages. I stood staring, amazed, but Jake started plucking things off the shelves left and right and shoving them into my arms.

"Stop gawking, Glory." He grinned. "Here. Here's some muffins. Doughnuts. Peanuts—good for protein. You should have some juice. Cheese slices." The amount of stuff he was loading me down with made me dizzy. Finally, when the pile I was holding was close to toppling over, he dragged me up to a counter, where a woman in a red apron and a pin on her shirt that said *Deborah* was leaning and fiddling with her nails.

"Will that be all?" she asked, looking straight at me.

Silence. I couldn't get up the nerve to reply.

"Yeah, that's it," Jake said, digging his elbow into my side. He cleared his throat. "Uh—you're sure Mom didn't want coffee?" he asked me.

I just stood there staring at him, dumbfounded. Finally I found the sense to nod, seeing what he was getting at—how we must have looked out of place here, on our own, in a place like this, at five in the morning. But the lady didn't seem to notice or care.

Jake pulled a wad of bills out of his pocket while the woman tap-tapped numbers into the contraption in front of her.

Money. I knew about money—from Jake, from Daddy—but I hadn't even thought of the money it would cost to get all this stuff. How would I ever be able to pay him back?

I felt a nudge on my shoulder. Deborah had loaded our food into bags and we were ready to go. I got into the truck,

Mookie practically licking my face off as I did. Jake fiddled with the gas box some more, then climbed into the driver's seat. And we were off again.

I must've nodded off somehow because suddenly the truck was stopped, and Jake was just sitting and staring at me. I sat up and looked around.

We were parked under some kind of bridge that ran across the road. There were no lights nearby that I could see, but the outlines of our surroundings stood out clearly. Dawn was on its way.

"We're not there, are we?" I asked. I'd been expecting more. Lights. Buildings. Fireworks. I don't know.

"We're just outside the town limits," he said. "This was the only place I could think of that'd be a good place for you to camp for now. I know it isn't much." He lifted his arms apologetically, indicating the bare landscape around him.

We all got out of the truck, and Jake led me under the bridge. "I found this nook before, once when I was little. My dad had pulled over so I could, uh, well, I couldn't hold it . . . and anyway, I remember seeing this place and thinking what a cool fort it would be. At least it'll keep you dry if it snows."

The nook he was talking about was a space under the bridge that was closed off on three sides by the same kind of material that was on the roads.

"I guess they used to use it to store roadwork equipment or something," Jake said.

I ducked inside the dark space and gave it a good once-over. It looked . . . well, miserable. The walls were covered in slime from the rainwater dripping down, and it smelled. I wondered if I wasn't the first one to be using it as a sleeping hut. But it was better than nothing.

I turned to Jake and gave him my best fake smile. "It's great!" I said lamely.

Jake's face was drawn and worried. He looked older, not so much like a boy but a man. I wondered if I still looked like a young girl or if all my suffering the past month showed in my face.

No matter. I gave Jake a hug, the first one I'd ever given him. "It's fine. It really is. Thank you."

Jake returned my hug awkwardly, then stepped back and looked me up and down. "You look good in my mother's clothes."

I moved into a pose like I'd seen on one of the girls from the magazines Jake had shown me. And I gave him a big magazine smile. We both laughed, but it was like we were making an effort.

"Let's unload your stuff," he said. We each carried a bag into the shelter and set it down in one corner. I made myself busy arranging everything. I laid down my coat to show Jake how cozy a bed I could make, but he appeared behind me with a blanket.

"My mom won't miss it," he said. He knelt down and spread it across the hard ground, bunching my knapsack up like a pillow at the top. "There. The lap of luxury."

We both stood there for a minute. Jake cleared his throat. I coughed. Mookie huffed.

"Okay, well. My dad'll be back early, so I've got to get going. You should try to sleep."

I nodded.

"Here's my address. And my number. And," he said, handing me a chunky, tightly folded piece of paper, "the address of a relative of mine in Shadow Tree, Rebecca Aiden. She's a second cousin. She owns a jewelry shop. I dunno how you feel about it, but you might want to look her up. She's real nice. Maybe you can do odd jobs for her or something. You know, stuff you could get paid for."

Odd jobs—for money? Something like that would be heavenly. I wondered why Jake hadn't told me about Rebecca before.

"I guess I was hoping I could change your mind," he said, like he had read my thoughts. "I mean, I didn't want to encourage you. But that was before, um, I knew how it was. Anyway, you still have to be careful. She might call the authorities if she finds out you're all alone."

"I'll be careful." I'd have to think about it—whether I'd approach Jake's cousin or not. I'd have to think about a lot of things tomorrow. Or rather, today.

He shuffled his feet. "Call me if you need anything."

"Okay."

"Okay, well . . ."

"Okay . . ."

Suddenly, Jake absorbed me in a giant hug. I felt the scratchy warmth of his shirt against my cheek and smelled his boy smell. A squeaky whine interrupted us.

I pulled back, wiping at my eyes, and bent down to give Mookie a hug. "I don't know when I turned into such a crybaby," I said, standing back up.

"You're not a crybaby." Jake punched me on the shoulder. "You're the toughest girl I've ever met. And I hear you can hit pretty hard." I laughed. We both laughed. I guess it was part of our bargain, to pretend that we weren't sad to say good-bye.

The first stranger I'd ever met disappeared in a blaze of red taillights (that's what they're called, you know) down the long, wide road outside of Shadow Tree, West Virginia. Watching him go, I felt like some invisible person, maybe God himself, had taken a pair of scissors and cut that long, thin elastic that had stretched from me, past Jake's house, through the long lonely woods, past my shelter made of sticks, all the way back to Dogwood.

Strangely, my heart didn't go with it—didn't snap straight out of my body like I'd thought it would. I was surprised to realize it was still beating inside me, still caring, suddenly missing Jake, still missing my family and home, always, always missing Katie, saying it was sorry over and over again.

But still, the elastic was broken. I was no longer connected.

Katie was still with me, my promises were still with me, my life was still with me—dwindling, but there. But home was in the past. I could never, ever, ever go back. I don't think I'd believed that really until I watched Jake drive away, back in the direction I'd come, down a road I'd never travel again.

When the last glimpses of the truck had vanished from my view, I let out a long, sorrowful sigh and looked at the folded paper I held in my hands. Absently I opened it, wanting to see Jake's handwriting, already missing him. As I did, a thick wad of green tumbled out and onto the ground. Money. I picked it up and counted it. Forty dollars. Amazed, I looked down the empty road, then back to the sheet of paper in my hands. Underneath his cousin's address, Jake had written a note: *G.—Don't count this on your log. Please. It's not all that much. I wish it was more. Call me if you need me.—J.*

I turned to face the bridge. Along the side where I was standing, a hill sloped steeply up to a plateau that ran level with the road above. I hurried to the base of the hill and scrambled up it, my shoes slipping and sliding in the snow to reveal dark mud underneath. Maybe I could still see him from here—maybe I could have a last look.

Finally I reached the top. I pulled myself up by the branch of a drooping pine and straightened my spine, looking, looking. But Jake was already gone. I was all alone. I turned back toward the slope. And then my breath caught in my throat.

To my right, stretched out in a patch of orange and yellow and white and even red lights, striped light and dark from the first rays of the sun and winking at me with all its modern shininess, was the town of Shadow Tree. The town was just beginning to rise—I could see miniature people walking, a few cars gliding along the streets, a man standing in front of his house waving to someone I couldn't see. I could even smell the scent of something warm and good being cooked, its aroma drifting my direction on the breeze.

Instinctively I wrapped my arms around myself. What on earth was a girl like me going to do in a town like this? In Dogwood, I'd always known where I was supposed to fit— even though I hadn't done a good job of doing it. Now I wondered, where was my place in a world like this? And if this was only a small town, where would my place be in a city like Boston? Would it swallow me up just like Jake had said?

I fingered the piece of paper Jake had given me, which was now in my pocket. Maybe I should call him. Maybe I could live out in his barn. Maybe, maybe, maybe.

But then I remembered that there was no maybe for me. There was only a definite ending. The poison that was part of my punishment was going to kill me no matter what I did— whether I exposed myself to the craziest folks of the outside world or hid out in a barn for the rest of my days. And that meant there was only one thing that could offer me any hope:

to enter this town, to find a way to earn my passage, to get to Boston and see it for Katie and me.

I would do it all. I would do it. I would. It was the only thing left to do.

"Bye," I said, to Mama and Daddy and my brother and sisters, and to the Reverend, and the Johansens, and to Jake and Mookie and the woods, and to dear, dear, dear home. "I love you."

I looked over the twinkling valley, and for the first time since the night that Katie died, I felt real, true hope.

There was a world beyond the world I knew. A new world. It was down there among the lights.

I took a step forward.

*Read the next installment
in Glory's dramatic adventure,*

SHADOW TREE

Standing on the outskirts of Shadow Tree, West Virginia, Glory faces one of the most frightening steps of her life—venturing into civilization. For the first time ever, she will be on her own in a strange and unfamiliar world.

A glance around the town makes it clear how different—and daunting—life outside of Dogwood is. Everything in Shadow Tree seems so full of hope. But Glory knows that if she is to keep her promise to Katie, she has to take this first step. Despite her fear, and the poison running through her veins, she's got to keep moving forward.

With no way of knowing who to trust and who to avoid, Glory will find herself taken in by some, and taken advantage of by others. But somehow, she must learn how to survive. Even though she might not have that much time left, she's not about to give up now. . . .